VIRAGO
MODERN CLASSICS
164

Barbara Comyns

Born in 1909 at Bidford-on-Avon, Barbara Comyns was educated mainly by governesses until she went to art schools in Stratford-upon-Avon and London. She started writing fiction at the age of ten and her first novel, *Sisters by a River*, was published in 1947. She also worked in an advertising agency, a typewriting bureau, dealt in old cars and antique furniture, bred poodles, converted and let flats, and exhibited pictures in The London Group. She was married first in 1931, to an artist, and for the second time in 1945. With her second husband she lived in Spain for eighteen years. She died in 1992.

Books by Barbara Comyns

Sisters by a River

Our Spoons Came from Woolworths

Who Was Changed and Who Was Dead

The Vet's Daughter

Out of the Red and into the Blue

The Skin Chairs

Birds in Tiny Cages

A Touch of Mistletoe

The Juniper Tree

Mr Fox

The House of Dolls

SISTERS BY
A RIVER

Barbara Comyns

Introduced by Barbara Trapido

virago

VIRAGO

First published in Great Britain by Eyre & Spottiswoode 1947
Published in paperback by Virago Press Limited in 1985
This edition published by Virago Press in 2013
Reprinted 2013, 2014

A CIP catalogue record for this book
is available from the British Library.

ISBN 978-1-84408-837-9

Typeset in Goudy by M Rules
Printed and bound in Great Britain by
Clays Ltd, St Ives plc

Papers used by Virago are from well-managed forests
and other responsible sources.

MIX
Paper from
responsible sources
FSC® C104740

Virago Press
An imprint of
Little, Brown Book Group
100 Victoria Embankment
London EC4Y 0DY

An Hachette UK Company
www.hachette.co.uk

www.virago.co.uk

INTRODUCTION

Anyone with a gothic streak will be gripped by this vivid auto-biographical novel about five sisters struggling to bring themselves up – with a high degree of ingenuity – as they dodge the fall-out created by their ill-matched and violent parents. In its entertaining portrayal of family life among the early twentieth-century servant-owning classes, the book is reminiscent of Nancy Mitford's *The Pursuit of Love*, though darker and edgier. For all its flair and its understated, childlike tone, for all its energy and fun and layered richness, the effect on the reader is unsettling. Adults, whether they be visiting aunts, grandmothers, governesses or parents, are as arbitrary and dangerous as tigers. Domestic servants are on the whole benign, but are dismissed (because their 'feet smelt') or end up in the workhouse.

Malevolence and the unexpected lurk around every corner in a story in which the house itself is an unpredictable character. Shellford Court is large and damp. An ancient pile dating from the 1500s, it is dominated by the river and smells of 'walnuts and church'. Despite its numerous rooms – boot room, engine room, billiards room, morning-room, drawing-room, along with its pantries, ante-rooms and cellars – it appears to afford our child narrator no fixed bedroom until, at fifteen, she and her older sister Beatrix are grudgingly permitted to inherit the room in which Granny has recently, grotesquely, died. The child, throughout her earlier years, will variously find herself evicted in the night from a dressing room by her screeching parents who are making fisticuffs, or accidentally bedded down beside a visiting male accountant, or waking up in Granny's bed to witness the old woman being rough-handled out of the window by her daughter and son-in-law. Wailing for her life, her nightdress bunched up to expose her crêpey old legs, Granny is saved from serious injury by the excessive width of her hips.

A younger sister is hurled downstairs as a baby because Daddy is fed up with her crying, and later misses her footing while sleepwalking and crashes down the same staircase. The house is prone to flooding, and the children have permanent coughs. They walk the garden on stilts. Bats threaten their uncombed hair. Rats emerge from the porridge. And the river, running past the door, inviting frequent escape, is itself pregnant with menace: a 'very dead boy' is discovered bumping about under Daddy's rowing boat; drowned pigs, bloated and rotting, are a common sight – a useful food source for the villagers, who whack the cadavers with sticks to cause an exodus of squirming edible eels.

But the major hazard for the novel's young narrator is other people, who, though violent, self-centred and bizarre, are depicted with a stoic, childlike acceptance and not a whiff of self-pity or exhibitionism. Comyns never had publication in mind and wrote the book as a private recollection: as solace for herself in difficult times and as a memoir for her children. Only when a friend came upon the manuscript in a suitcase was she persuaded to offer it for publication. And then, since it didn't quite fit the soothing picture of childhood favoured in post-war stories, it was repeatedly rejected until it was serialised in *Lilliput* magazine under the provoking title, 'The Novel Nobody Will Publish'. In 1947, the publishing house Eyre & Spottiswoode took a chance on it – six years after she wrote it – by which time Comyns had completed the better-known *Our Spoons Came From Woolworths*. She went on to produce a total of ten brave, alluring and highly original novels during the course of an eventful life in which she married twice, exhibited her paintings, bred poodles, managed a garage, renovated apartments and sold antique furniture. A reader would expect no less from a person who had survived the baptism of fire depicted within the pages of *Sisters by a River*.

Daddy proposes to Mammy when she is still a child. He will marry her, he says, on condition that she learns how to cook, and this she certainly does. All the enjoyable family interludes in this story of eye-boggling neglect and abuse have to do with food: Christmas is a marvellous extravaganza, as are the picnics, the dinner parties, the tennis parties. Mammy starts childbearing at eighteen, and stops only when her sixth confinement renders her both infertile and stone deaf. By turns hostile and indifferent to her children, and given to lines such as, 'How I wish I'd never had you . . . I hate you all,' she is an unstable, self-indulgent and spiteful woman, whose rare attempts at maternal closeness are both alarming and weird. She talks out loud to imaginary lovers and uses her children as go-betweens in her ongoing war with Daddy.

Daddy, rumoured among the servants to have a 'touch of the Tarbrish', is a petulant rage machine. Brooding upon his debts, and seeking solace in too much whisky, he is constantly infuriated by the presence of his wife, his mother-in-law and his children – though he is always at one with Palmer, the gardener, an odious and cruel tyrant who severs the heads of newborn kittens. Daddy, on one occasion, knocks Mammy about so brutally that she's obliged to lurk indoors, a white-faced ghost in hiding from her own garden party, and he horsewhips his daughter into near-unconsciousness in reprimand for a minor mishap with a breakfast egg. He blasts his ancient cat into a gory splatter of dispersed body parts, and stalks the passages, revolver in hand, ready for bailiffs and tax inspectors. But he and Mammy come together in vanity, being much occupied by their social position. Daddy requires the entire household to witness the finesse of his once-a-month departures on business to Birmingham: getting ready takes him three hours. He adores his boot collection and has 'a room lined with shelves all filled with beautiful shiny shoes'; for his buttonhole he favours an out of season bloom, which causes 'a great comb out of the greenhouses'. 'Although we live in the country, we are cultured,' Mammy declares to her ill-educated, badly dressed daughters, with their rotting teeth. 'Not many girls have your opportunities.' Meanwhile, Granny, a one-time femme fatale, has metamorphosed over the years into a hideous bad fairy, a blown-up compulsive eater who terrorises the maids and repels her granddaughters, bawling commands from her bedroom, which is sticky with mint humbugs, old hair and 'rotting sealskin jackets'.

Added to the adult menace is the monstrous rule of Mary, the eldest of the girls, who is left unchecked to oppress and bully her siblings. None is permitted to read a book that Mary likes, which rules out *The Wind in the Willows* along with a range of childhood favourites. None is permitted to wear a garment in any colour but brown because Mary has the monopoly on brightness and style; the sisters endure hours of shame as dowdy outcasts, spurned and humiliated at dances and hunting parties. Beyond the immediate family, there is a cavalcade of demented and mean-minded relations, from the aunt with 'seal flapper' feet, who washes the meat in disinfectant, to Daddy's youngest sister, the intermittently incarcerated 'aunt with the square face', who can't touch anything once it's been touched by somebody else. And then there are the villagers, who are variously macabre, exotic, malformed, retarded or merely wretched.

In spite of the minefield of lunacy and violence that they are forced to negotiate, the sisters exhibit an imaginative richness, being mostly left alone to invent games and rituals, to dismiss their own governess, to inhabit orchards and verdant secret spaces, to eat honey from the comb, to navigate the river with its abundance of fish. Unsurprisingly, they also exhibit signs of disturbance and stress: nightmares and chattering teeth, sleepwalking and nervous tics. Theirs is a world that is tinged with the surreal and the macabre: Beatrix and Barbara levitate, riding on a magic branch that carries them over the rooftops (that's until Mary deliberately breaks the branch); they observe an enchanting rain of hats that fills the sky, just as if they were inside a Magritte painting; Barbara meets God in the billiards room; Chloe burns all her things and rips the heads off dolls. In addition, the girls visit horrible cruelties on animals: they hang caterpillars from miniature gallows and 'resurrect' moths over candle flames.

And then, one day, it's all gone: the furniture gone under the hammer; Mammy despatched to a grim, ill-appointed cottage; the children dispersed. All is swept away. Yet it's all here, on the page, thanks to the flair and recall of its talented chronicler; something for which every reader will be grateful.

Barbara Trapido, 2013

SISTERS BY
A RIVER

Being Born

It was in the middle of a snowstorm I was born, Palmer's brother's wedding night, Palmer went to the wedding and got snowbound, and when he arrived very late in the morning he had to bury my packing under the wallnut tree, he always had to do this when we were born – six times in all, and none of us died, Mary said Granny used to give us manna to eat and that's why we didn't, but manna is stuff in the bible, perhaps they have it in places like Fortnham & Mason, but I've never seen it, or maybe Jews shops.

Mammy rather liked having babies, it was one of the few times she was important and had a fuss made of her, but Granny used to interfeer a lot, and an old woman called Mrs Basher who lived in a round cottage used to come too, but she didn't when I was born because of the snow.

Daddy got dreadfully annoyed about all these babies coming all the time, he said it was a conspiricy to ruin him. He got quite fond of us as we grew older, at least he sometimes was, and used to take us mushrooming on our bycicles early in the mornings and we would stop at Heath's farm to drink new

3

warm milk, he gave us each a garden and taught us to row, so he must have liked us.

The first thing I can remember is being in a white pram by a lot of ivy and it started to rain but not on me, the rain ended in a straight line which gradualy came nearer, just as it reached me someone in blue came running out of the house and took me in.

The next thing I can remember was Kathleen being born and I wasn't the baby any more, I was not allowed in the pram and how my legs used to ache on the long walks the maids used to take us. We didn't have proper nurses with vails, like the Crawfords, except once when we had a beautiful one who wore pink and had a wide stiff belt, but Granny made her go away because she washed the nappies with sticks. Our nursery was very dark with fir trees pushing in at the windows, but we were seldom in it. There was a wonderful picture on the wall of a girl in a wood stiff with bluebells and white rabbits and ducks, but when I saw the picture again some years later, they were all rabbits and no ducks atall, I think I was about two before I could see what picturs were meant to be, sometimes I don't know even now.

There are lots of vague memories floating around my mind of when I was very young, some are comfortable like driving in a closed carriage with Auntie Eva and Granny all dressed in black and nodding plums in their hats, a tiny dog called Fido, we stopped at a cottage to get him a drink, I saw him lapping out of a saucer with a gold rim, I went to sleep and when I awoke there was an old woman with a basket full of bananas at the carriage door, they gave me one and it was nice, I eat it

4

and went to sleep again, it was very warm. But there are other memories that make me think I would hate to be a small child again, being left strapped in an awful little chair with a pot in it, being left for simply hours and being left in the bath till the water had gone quite cold, and being frightened in the night, and falling down stairs, we were always doing that, and of course being smacked, though we weren't smacked much before we were three. After three everything seems clearer, almost clearer than things had happened yesterday.

Mary – the eldist

Mary was the eldist of the family, Mammy was only eighteen when she had her, and she was awfully frit of her, but Daddy thought she was lovely and called her his little Microbe, I don't know why, maybe microbes were just coming into fashion then like we have germs now. When Daddy came home in the evening Mary had to be woken up and taken down stairs, and almost every day she had a new toy, and she was always being taken to the photographer. But by the time she was three or four there were such a lot of babies no one bothered about her any more. Mammy said the first words she ever said were 'I'm so miserable' and I expect she was. Mary was the plainest in the family, but she made up for it by being so bossy. I have often noticed the eldist in a family isnt so pretty as the others, usually the youngest is the best, it is so in fairy stories too, it must be because the parents havn't had enough practice at making babies.

Mary was frightfully domoneering to us all including Mammy, I cant think why she bothered about us so much, jeleousy perhaps, if a friend of hers came to the house we were not allowed to speak to them, we could only wear clothes of a colour she choose for us, she said I was only to wear brown – beastly brown, because my eyes were brown, how tierd I got of brown. Another crazy thing, we were not allowed to read any book she liked, there was a list, *Green Mansions*, *The Wind in the Willows*, W. H. Davis's poems, John Drinkwater, etc. I felt quite guilty when I read *The Wind in the Willows* the other day.

Mary wouldn't go for walks with us because she said we were a Tribe and our clothes were a disgrace to her, and our dogs were mongerals and behaved abombably. On the whole she wasn't so filthy to me, except about the awful brown clothes, but Beatrix had a frightful time – worse after she left school, I think her violin playing got on her nerves. Poor Kathleen and Chloe were bullied and nagged all day, she was always discovering they had dirty ears, or had forgotten to put their knickers on, sometimes it was how badly they spoke or that they couldn't tell the time when they were twelve. After she left school she would try and teach them long poems by Scott about 'Young Locinvar coming out of the West' and they would cry and say they wished they were dead, but fortunatly Mary tierd of any new project, and she would forget Kathleen and Chloe and how neglected they were, and lots of books on bees would come, bees never were a success for long in our family, but hives and Queen excluders and all kinds of queer things would arrive, finally bees, but she was much too timid to go near them, and later on too bored and they just swarmed away. Then it was Angora rabbits, she was going to make a fortune out of their combings, the coach house would be filled with large sacks simply stuffed with beautiful white wool. Two

7

pedigree Angoras arrived and it seemed as if a fortune actually was forthcoming, they increased so quickly, after a few weeks Kathleen and Chloe were told they must do the combing, and after a day or two even they, browbeaten as they were went on strike, so the rabbits coats or is it pelts got more and more matted and their hutches smelt simply awful, then they wern't fed and started excaping, the dogs killed some and bit the legs off others, so the survivers were let loose in the woods and that was the end of them.

Then there was a farming craze, Mary went to a farm every day, but we wern't allowed near, we thought it the best craze she had had and she didn't interfer with us atall.

When Mary grew up and we were all parted she completely changed and was always pleased to see us and remembered our birthdays and was helpful when we were in trouble, although for years her own life was a sad one.

Early days of a Batchlor Girl

Next to Mary in our family was a child I shall never mention in this book, because I know they would hate to appear in it, after this mystery child came Beatrix, she was quite unlike the rest of us both in appearance and nature. She was rather like the Dresden china women who lived in the drawingroom cabinates, her skin was much fairer than ours and freckles came on her arms, we teased her about this, also her forehead was quite narrow, the rest of the family had rather bulgy foreheads, high cheek bones and very far apart eyes, everyone said she looked like Granny, but Granny had a great chin jutting out. Beatrix used to stay clean, she didn't get all black round her mouth like we did, and her hair was straight and didn't have bits of twig and knots in it like ours, of course the dirt and twigs used to come off us in the bath. The governesses used to like Beatrix, at night they would roll her hair up in curling rags. We used to sleep in the same bed for years and hated it, Beatrix always said I had more than my half and fixed an awful brass rod down the bed so that I didn't take more than my share, she was always worrying in case she had not had her fair share of something or that she had been unjustly treated. Beatrix's clothes used to stay neat and tidy, as she grew older she always mended her stockings and gloves, I used to mend my stockings with pieces of stiff grass threaded in and out. Beatrix and I always played together and were good friends on the whole until she went to boarding school with Mary, then she came back very changed, she was even neater in her dress and she had got all religious, it wore off a little as the holidays progressed. When she left school Mary used to nag and bully her and she would shut herself up in the billiard room and play the gramophone beating time with a pencil. Once a week she would go to Evesham to have violin lessons, I used to think it must be wonderful to go out in the world like this, poor girl she had no friends and nothing to do all day except scrape away on her violin, after Daddy died she went away with a beastly old great aunt and learnt to be a secretary and became a batchlor girl with a flat.

Babies Arriving

A nurse called Maud was dressing me, she made me stand on a chair by the open nursery door, I could see Mary running down the landing, she wore a white frock and black stockings, I could see her garters, she was very excited and put her head through the door and said 'Mammy has hatched a new baby in the night' and ran on to tell the others. Maud said 'Has she now, just fancy that, well Miss you wont be the baby any more.' I didn't want to be the baby anyway, and was glad someone elce would have to be the youngest now. It was quite true about the new baby, later on we went to see it, and Daddy took a photograph of us all standing round the frilly cot, the baby was Kathleen.

It seemed just a few weeks later and Chloe arrived, Beatrix and I had noticed Mammy was looking rather queer, but we thought she had been eating a lot of gravy, I wouldnt eat any more in case I got all lumpy too, she had to sit on a strange rubber ring at meal times. We didn't like Chloe very much, she was rather large and had a fat mauve face and cried dreadfully. Until she was about five she was a dull lumpy child, with rather buldging blue eyes, people said she was like an owl, then she suddenly changed and started to show signs of great beauty, at sixteen she was the most beautiful girl I have ever seen, extreemely tall and slender, with great black plates hanging far below her waist, and a lovely misterious face.

The day Chloe was born there was great excitement in the village, an aeroplain was going to fly over the village, following the river, it was the first time anyone we knew had seen one, most of the village gathered on the bridge, which was a very fine Normon one, so bore their weight without complaint, we waited in one of the points with Miss Vann, Mammy had to see it from her bedroom window. All the people started to shout and point, 'There it is, there it is, just like a great bird' in their excitement some of their hats fell in the river, I followed the pointing hands with my eyes, there was a dark little thing like a crow miles away in the sky, I ran to the other side of the bridge, there were the hats just coming through, I was disapointed with the aeroplain but no one else was.

As if she had No Ears at all

After she had had six babies at eighteen monthly intervals Mammy suddenly went deaf, perhaps her subconcious mind just couldn't bear the noise of babies crying any more. One night soon after Chloe was born, she woke up and instead of hearing a baby crying, all she could hear was a rushing sound, right in her head, she tried talking to herself but couldn't hear her voice, then she banged on the wall, all she heard was the dreadful rushing noise, so she started to scream and woke every one up. They all came running to her room, they opened and shut their mouths but that was all, she was quite deaf as if she had no ears at all, and she never heard again. She was taken to several specialists but they could do nothing, one good thing being deaf stopped her having any more babies, she was only twenty seven and might have had masses more, somehow being deaf put a stop to them.

Mammy had always looked and been rather vague, she had a kind of gypsoflia mind, all little bits and pieces held together by whisps, now she grew vaguer still and talked with a high floating voice, leaving her sentences half finished or

13

with a wave of her hand she would add an 'and so forth' which was a favourite expression. Sometimes when she was showing visitors round the garden she would suddenly come upon us playing some wierd game, she would look quite startled as if she had never seen us before and say something like this 'The children, grubby, playing dont you know, such a number of them, I married very young, quite a nice governess' and hurry her guests away, which was just as well because we had rather abomonable manners and used to make loud remarks about any stranger 'Oh what an ugly old woman, she has got china teeth, and they wobble' but if they were pretty, which was very unusual, all five of us would follow quite enchanted and pester them to look at our scars, hear how bad our coughs were or how many teeth we had missing, and they had to see all our dogs, puppies, kittens, mice, catterpillers and snails.

Mammy seemed to loose all contact with us, we never looked on her as a real person, she seldom did anything for us, and if she did she was very selfconscious about it and made us feel all shy, when she talked to us, she would use a special voice, sometimes she would suddenly say 'Come and kiss me' we were awfully embarrised when she did this as we were not at all demonstrative and when she felt that way Mammy was very sentermental, other times she would be very fierce and spiteful, though she seldom hit us, she would say 'How I wish I'd never had you, I never wanted all these children' or 'You are just like your father, I hate you all' After she had one of these moods she would come and sit on our beds and cry, we would wake up and find her there, and it would be awful.

Other times she hardly noticed us at all, and that was the most peaceful.

As soon as we learnt how to spell we talked to Mammy on our hands, and grew very quick at it, faster than we could talk with our mouths, when Daddy was angry which was rather frequent, he used to spell every word out loude, then repeating the word 'NO no I I HAVNT havnt ANY any BLOODY bloody MONEY money FOR for THE the BLOODY bloody MAIDS maids SACK sack THE the LOT lot' that would come floating or rather thundering out of the billiard room windows and we knew Mammy was asking for the servants wages.

It must have been beastly looking at all those flapping hands all the time, if you tried to tell her something she didnt want to hear or that she did not agree with she would turn her head away and refuse to look at your hands.

Some of the local people learnt deaf and dumb language too, but usually they used little pads that were put in every room, it was quite amusing to read the one sided, jerky conversations after they had left

Would you be kind enough to lend me your steriliser
Yes, Monday would do, so many plumbs this year
The locum seems so nice, pity its only a month, unmarred too
Yes she is very thin, delicate mothers have them at such a rate
You should get your mother to wear pygamas, so warm
I never allowed my girls to do it, send it on Monday.

15

I found a piece of paper in an old book with all that on, and it was typical of the drawing-room pad any afternoon.

Later on we had waxed tablets people had to write on, you wrote on them with an orange stick, when you pulled it all the writing dissapeared, Mammy perfered these, she said people said more interesting things on them

Granny

Grannies bedroom smelt of toilet vinager, she used to wash her face in it to prevent wrinkles, she certainly had an almost unlined face, but maybe it wasn't due to toilet vinager, just will power or something, because her hair was still brown, and it was not vinager but bay rum she put on that. Her bedroom was in the most awful mess with all her toilet preperations and the homemade medicines she brewed there, embrocations for horses legs 'Oilevambor' to rub on our chests in the winter and goose oil too, and bottles of homemade wine all gone sour, the carpet was all stuck up with stuff she had spilt, if you walked over it with your bare feet, your feet would hardly come away from the stickiness. All her drawers were stiff with junk, spilt fullers earth, and everything all tangled up with hair nets, bits of cotton wool and sweets, the wardrobe and cupboards were stuffed with impossible clothes, feather boas and plumed hats, rotting sealskin jackets, broken toys and pillow cases full of old letters, she guarded all this rubbish with great fierceness and couldn't bear anyone to go into her room in case they looked in her drawers or stole something, she was

17

always accusing the maids of prying or stealing her peper-mints. But Granny was not always a messy old woman, when she was young she had many admirers, I think she had eight-een proposals of marrage, she was not beautiful, but had great personality and was a fameous horsewoman, when she was a child Queen Victoria saw her riding in the Row and had her included in a painting she had commissioned of Rotten Row, her father had many paintings done of her riding enormouse horses either jumping hedges or leaping brooks, her riding habit blowing about in graceful folds. All this made her grow very spoilt and willful, and unfortunately in a fit of peque (that is what she always said or is that a kind of material) she married the least worthy of her suiters; a weak charming man who spent most of his time and Grannies money looking for gold in America, he must have come home sometime because he had seven stillborn sons and my mother, at least Granny had them. Granny never talked about him much, but you could tell she didn't like him, I do remember her saying he was a very impatient man and if his shirts were startched too stiff or were difficult to get into he would tear them to shreds. In the end when he had got no more money left he had to walk accross America and come home steerage, when he got home he had a heart attack and was dead. Granny didn't mind much, Mammy was about five at the time, and after his death spent most of her time at Hillersdon with Gt Grand Daddy and Aunt Eva, she said she hated to have to go home, they were rather poor and the house was always in the most fright-ful mess, Granny would trail with cans of water to the greenhouse, her long skirts swishing in the pools she left behind her, she did no housework or cooking, all that was left to some little overworked skivvy, who never had an evening off because she was so scared of Jack the Ripper. Her pride wouldn't let her return to her family, although she frequently sent frantic letters saying she was in bed, ill and helpless, but when Aunt Eva hurried to her bedside there was usually nothing the matter at all. It was odd that she didn't remarry, as she was not very old when her husband died and still quite good looking and considered to be very witty and amusing, but perhaps her violent temper and the muddle the house was in scared away possible husbands.

After a time she moved to a house that belonged to my father, only he wasn't my father then, one day he came to the house about something, probably no rent had been paid for simply ages, as he came up the garden path he saw Mammy trying to skip, she was making an awful mess of it, getting all tangled up in the rope, but he thought she looked very nice so he said 'When you grow up I will marry you ask your Mother to teach you how to cook' He bought her a goat and a white kitten to remember him by, but the goat burst and the kitten was run over by a train, all the same she did marry him just before she was eighteen, she also learnt how to cook, from Aunt Eva I expect, when she was twelve she cooked a complete five course dinner for Daddies benifit, he was pleased with her for remembering what he had told her to do. But the Hillersdon people were not at all pleased when they discovered Granny had married her off like that, they did not consider Daddy at all suitable and they were annoyed that Granny had kept him a secret all those years, the only thing to reccomend him was that he was rich, they never had Granny to the house again and Daddy only went there once.

Mammy had no honeymoon, she went straight to Daddy's dark, ugly house stuffed with Edwardian furniture and red plush also stuffed birds in glass cases, Granny came with her, there were also two of his sisters living there, the eldest had been doing the housekeeping, she was an extreemly domoneering spiteful woman, small and dark like a beetle, the other sister was the youngest of the family and a bit batty, she didn't resent Mammy so much. The first months of her married life must have been grim, eventually Daddy tierd of being surrounded by bickering, posessive women, so he sent his sisters off to Folkestone where they stayed until they were dead. Mammy still had her mother to quarrel with, some women like having their mothers to live with them but Mammy just hated it, Daddy was quite fond of her, they were more of an age and really got on very well, much better than Mammy and Daddy did really. After two babies were born, they moved to Shellford Court and of course Granny came too, just to settle her daughter in, but she stayed there for ever more, but she was very useful with the babies, and kind to us when we were small, I expect a few of us would have died or drowned if it hadn't been for her. She used to tell us the most wonderful stories about her life in Ireland and tales she had been told when she was a child, when she talked she made things seem so vivid, it was the same when we played games with her, we would play shops with leaves when we were in the garden, if she said a bay leaf was a humbug, and an oak leaf a pound of tea, the leaves seemed to turn into a humbug and a pound of tea in front of our eyes. She had a great old gray coat, we would say she was a gray hen and we were the chickens under her wings. As we grew older she became impatient with us and we got on her nerves rather a lot, but we used to think she was nice once and try not to annoy her too much. All our family were very supersticious, but Granny was the worst, and she was always seeing spirits about the house, when the wind blew in the pine trees at night and made a schreeching howling sound she said it was the restless spirits crying, but I am sure it was the trees, and she would say things about the house had a curse on them, even our toys and they were burnt because of that, sometimes I thought maybe she was a witch in rather thin disguise.

Granny was pretty filthy to the maids, she always thought of them as a kind of slave and said they were disloyal if they had an evening out, she was grim to the governesses too. Once she mesmerised one of the maids and made her climb into the pigsty and kiss the pig, she didn't mesmerise us.

When I was about four I can remember a rather dreadful thing happening, it was very early in the morning and for some reason I had been put to sleep in the same bed as Granny, but I woke up and found she wasn't in bed but walking up and down the room with her jaw all sticking out muttering to herself, she kept saying 'I wont have it, I wont have it' I sat up in bed and said 'What won't you have a jam tart' in my imagination I could see a criss cross rasberry one, but she said 'Don't be so impertanant' so I didn't like to say anything else, but she kept marching up and down in her long white nighty and it got rather boring, I was almost asleep again, when there was a frightful din about the room, Daddy, Mammy and Granny were all shouting and moping and mowing, then Mammy and Daddy started to push the poor old thing out of the window, Mammy got a bit frit and started to scream, but it was dreadful to see Daddy pushing and heaving away and Granny getting more and more out of the window, there were awful ghaspings and groanings going on from Granny and her flapping white nighty was all up at the back which seemed to make it worse somehow, Mammy looked quite sad, I guess she felt quite sorry for her when she was half in and half out like that, then she got stuck, it really was a mercy her hips were so wide and the window rather narrow, no one was noticing me so I got out of bed and ran and hid in the apple room, but it was the wrong time of year for apples so very dreary there. Granny did not appear till lunch time, and everything seemed the same as usual then, her eyes were rather red maybe and she didn't talk quite as much as usual but she eat masses of chicken and it was only boiled, when Daddy said 'Have a little more Nance' she handed up her plate quite happily.

As she became older food became the chief joy of her life, she never went out at all and usually retired to her room when visitors came, so life was rather dull for her, soon after breakfast she would say 'Run to the kitchen and ask the maids what we are having for lunch dear' but the maids in the midst of their work would say 'Oh tell the old woman its boiled beef and carrots' A little later in the morning she would sniff with her straight, pinched nose and murmur 'It doesn't smell like boiled beef to me, just slip into the kitchen and open the oven door very gently and see if there is a little duck roasting inside, I could just fancy a nice duckling with sage, onions and green peas' The jingle of table laying was Grannies favourite music now, I do hope I am dead before I'm old.

The Aunt with the Square Face

We had an aunt and she went mad, Aunt Minnie was her name, she was Daddies youngest sister. She had a square face and thought everyone was dirty and wouldn't touch anything anyone else had touched, money or a train ticket, almost anything you can think of, she took her own knives and forks when she had a meal away from home and washed them up herself, Mammy said she used a cake of soap every day, in the end she got so mad she was sent to a home, she took her own sheets and bedclothes and all kinds of things with her. After some time had passed she got less batty so they let her loose again. All the things she had used there were packed in huge black trunks and sent to our house to be thrown in the river, she said she couldn't bear to see anything she had used when shut up. Daddy didn't bother to have them drowned, they were just put in a dark corner of the coach house and forgotten for years. Then Mary, Beatrix and I found them and had a lovely time, there was a patchwork quilt and a diamond ring, Mary had that and sold it after Daddy was dead, we knew it was a diamond because it cut glass. Beatrix had a cumpas and some other things like that, but I had a beautiful doll with a wax head and a bustle, she was almost as large as me, I called her Minnie, I left it in the maids lav and Coddy Bennet-the-muck-man took her away.

After we went back to school and Beatrix got all religious again she wrote home and confessed what she had done, the grown-ups didn't mind they took all the useful things like sheets out of the trunks and used them, but Minnie didn't know because she hardly ever came to our house. When she did come it was with her sister who looked like a black beetle, she – the black beetle one used to go in the kitchen and find all that waste going on, then she would go and tell Daddy, but it wasn't much good because he only minded the waste on quarter day.

Mammy used to invite the Hillersdon relations over to see how awful Daddy's sisters were, when they had gone Mammy would say Aunt Teana thinks Lizzie and Minnie are simply frightful, then there would be a row, sometimes the Aunts left before their visit was really over. I feel rather sad for them when I think what dreary lives they had.

The Rolly Polly Field

A girl with a mauve facce and long plats looked over the hedge
and all the cows started dashing about all over the field, it was
one of those fields full of roly-poly hills caused by ploughing
hundreds of years ago I believe. The cows tore up and down
the hills and the girl with the mauve face dissapeared, then the
cows noticed us going for our daily walk with Miss Vann, so
they started charging at us instead, we all ran for the style,
Mary and Beatrix got there first, then Miss Vann with her
black specticals on the end of her nose, but a frightful, speck-
ely cow had picked on me and each time I got on top of a hill
I couldn't help stooping and looking at it through my legs, it
looked simply dreadful like that, Miss Vann kept shreaking
instructions to me but she didn't come and help, just as I felt
its hot smoky breath on my back, the farmer called Heath
dashed out of a shed and threw his coat over its head and I was
saved. For a long time after I was frit of cows and the family
dispised me.

Some time later we had a rather frightful governess called
Tucker, she didn't have a very long reign, one day when she

26

was taking us for a walk to Marlcliff, we found a landslide made of clay, so we all slid down on our bottoms and couldnt get up again, at least we pretended we couldn't, so Miss Tucker got all angry and flustered and eventually had to slide down too. When we started walking home we had to pass through a field of great snorting cows, Mary and Beatrix just went on, but I just refused to, poor Miss Tucker tried to drag me but I spat at her, then she suddenly sat down and started crying. I felt horrofied, there she sat on the grass all huddled up, she wore a huge hat of very corse straw, like a giant biscuit, ever since she came I had been longing to bite it but had not had the chance, so I said 'If you will let me bite your hat I'll go through that awful field' so I bit her hat, you could hardly tell anyone had had a bite out of it, then we went through the field and I felt so brave I touched one of the cows and it took no notice, so I was never frightened of them again.

God in the Billard Room

The billard room belonged to Daddy, like the potting shed was Palmers, he wasn't supposed to be disturbed in there and it was only cleaned on Mondays when he had gone to Birmingham, Mammy and one of the maids took an enormous patent cleaner called the 'Daisy Vacume Organ' two people had to work it and it was almost as large as a barrel organ, but supposed to be very labour saving. The Billardroom had only been build recently, and was huge – rather like an awful church, there was a large stained window from the floor to the ceiling at one end of the room, the only other window looked into a conservotry, and did not open, you could just see masses of green through, and made me feel like a fish in a pond. There was a funny light in the billard room, and I wasn't really surprised when one hot sunny morning I walked in there to get cool and there was God, he was over by the fishy window and just glided up to me, I knew it was God although he looked like an enormous parchment coloured bag drawn up round the neck with cord, I had been expecting to see Him for a long time but I couldn't help being rather overcome and fainted.

When the grown ups found me they wouldn't believe I had seen God and I fainted rather a lot after that so they said I mustn't eat crab, and I still don't and I've never seen Him any more.

There were lots of dusty mooses head handing around the dark imatitation panneled walls and some frightful paintings of dogs burning themselves with boiling water and of race horses like skeletons; the opersite end of the room to the stained glass window was an alcove with a red plush couch in it, this was heaped in old fur rugs, that had a fascinating musty bitter smell, but I expect most people would think they smelt simply awful, there was a rainbow painted on the arch above the alcove, it looked rather misplaced. In the large window was Daddy's writing desk, he wrote masses of letters, not important ones, but he just liked writing, posting the letters was rather an official thing, Palmer had to do it, if you wrote a letter you had to leave it on the billardroom table to be stamped.

In the evenings, particularly Saturday, the Old Doctor and the handsome Doctor used to come and play billards with Daddy, also the vicar, they used to drink whiskey and eat Huntley & Palmers ginger biscuits too, it was rather reassuring if there seemed to be a ghost in the room to hear the click of billard balls and men laughing in the distance.

There was a thing we rather liked in there called the cinafonium or something, a kind of giant musical box, which played three records at once, also we had a gramophone with a huge green horn, when we played it we used to wrap ourselves up in the fur rugs.

Rooted to the Ground

I guess I must have got rooted to the ground like they say in books, it didn't last for very long but all the same it was grim while it did, but poor Beatrix, it must have been far worse for her, there she was screaming like one of Palmers pigs and I couldn't move my legs an inch to run and get help. My hands were behind me and there they stayed, just tearing up some poppies I'd been picking before the awfull thing had happened. All I could do was look at Beatrix, and hear those screams, her leg was getting all pinched and crushed between the heavy folding garden seat, that somehow had collapsed on her, her pink leg just seemed to end half way down and I had a feeling the unseen half must have fallen off the other side of the pinching wood, but in my mind I could see it, all stiff and bloody still wearing its shoe and sock. She had been screaming for a very long time or so it seemed to me, by now they were growing rather fainter though, and my feet were getting more and more rooted to the ground, but just as I thought now I really am turning to stone or salt like Lots wife, there came Daddy running across the lawn, all dressed in the whitest white flapping nightshirt and his face covered in fluffy shaving soap, his mastarche showing all black and huge. Soon he had freed her, and she lay very limp in his arms, the awfull leg hung down, thin in the middle then very fat again like a wasps waist but it still hung together. I tried to move my feet to follow them and they came away from the ground, they were so heavy like great weights and as I dragged them along they tingled and pricked but I had to follow to see if Beatrix's leg fell off before they got to the house, I hobbled along after them and kept them in sight all the time but it didn't.

Rooms

The drawing-room smelt a bit musty and Victorian but we, with the exception of Mary thought it the most beautiful room in the world. It was built at a later period than the main part of the house, which went back to fifteen something, most of the rooms were small and low ceilinged, so the drawing-room appeared to be particularly large to us. The furniture was made of some shiny black wood with short bow legs, rather like mine, the upholstery was of pale blue brocade embossed with lovers knots and the carpet was pale blue with more lovers knots, it was all rather worn and faided when you looked into it. Of course the wall paper was the silvery stripey kind that I was always meeting on other peoples drawing-room walls in those days decorated by washed out water colour landscapes, usually painted by an aunt. There was a chandelier hanging down from the middle of the ceiling, during Spring cleaning it was taken to pieces and each piece washed separately, it took a long time to put it together again, there was a high white marble mantlepiece rather stiff with china, so were several cabinets, some of it was good and rather nice, the rest pretty awful. Strange feathered relics were scattered about, among them was a stuffed swan fire-screen, also rather a frightening owl with extended wings standing on a drumstick, this one was supposed to use to shield your face from the fire, no one used it, perhaps because it smelt a bit strong.

A piano stood facing the wall, and for good reason, it was backed by pale blue satin liberaly embroidied with ribbon, (Aunt Lizzie's work) a nude alabaster woman sitting on a drainpipe lived on top. Every drawing-room I entered in those days seemed to have French windows leading into a conservatory, and so did ours, I think they were meant for people to propose in, but I never heard anyone do so in ours.

We really prefered to use the morning-room, as it was more comfortable and warmer, there was an enormouse arm chair for Daddy, a slightly smaller, harder chair for Mammie and a perfectly round chair, like a little plush table for Granny, because she liked to sit with her feet all tucked under her, there wern't enough chairs for all of us, there never were, except in the dining-room, which was a kind of forest of table and chairs, so we used to sit about on the floor, I just can't sit in armchairs now, I'm never really comfortable unless I am sitting on the floor.

The morning-room was a bit fierce till you got used to it, there was nearly always an overpoweringly hot fire, scarlet walls, scarlet carpet and at one time scarlet upholstery, there were some good sporting prints on the walls, but one was usually too dazzeled to see them properly and some of the furniture that wasn't scarlet was old and rather beautiful, on a chest

33

there were two of the largest pewter plates I have ever seen, they looked good in the firelight.

Jimmy-the-Dog lived under Granny's chair, he was always growling to himself, Merrythought the small squirrel monkey used to sit over the fire or climb about the curtains that had pictures of monkeys climbing up them, they were about the same size as he was. The window was never opened in winter so it didn't smell exactly fresh, but was very cosy, the fire grate was usually littered with chestnut shells, cigarette ends and Merrythought's banana skins, there were books, newspapers and magazenes every where.

Both the morning-room and dining-room opened onto a long veranda which someone had added to the house, there used to be a swing in it once but I somehow managed to swing right through a glass door and although the door was smashed to bits I wasnt hurt in the least, all the same they removed the swing to a tree by the river.

When I was very young I could hardly ever tell which was the dining-room and which the morning-room if I was looking at them from the garden, I had the same trouble distinguishing between gold and silver and strangly, Mammie and Granny, I cant think how that came about, they were very different in appearance, Beatrix used to say, 'You are stupid, Granny is the one who wears specticals when she reads' but it wasn't much help when she wasn't reading.

It Wasn't Nice in the Dressing Room

Often we woke in the night to hear Mammies rather crupy laughter, when she remembered something that amused her, something that happened even years ago, she laughed and laughed, it was rather frightening to hear laughter like that in the black night, maybe she didn't realize how awful it sounded, being deaf, but if you slept in the dressing room you wished she wouldn't. There were worse things that happened when you slept there, although it was thought by Mammy to be a privaledge to sleep in the dressing room. Some nights there would be a frightful noise coming from the next room, angry voices and slamming doors, then Mammy would appear, sieze you out of bed and say 'For heavens' sake find somewhere elce to sleep, run along to your Granny'. You would be pushed out and the door locked behind you, sometimes I would wait out side hoping the door would open again, usually only sobbing and muttering came out, so the only thing would be to creep down the creaking stairs and lonely landing and go to the first room you came to, once I did this and found myself the next morning in bed with a dreadful old man who smelt of lead pencils, he was an accountant was came to stay once a year to help Daddy get out of his income tax.

There were two quite good things about the dressing-room, one of them was there were a lot of lady birds in there every summer, they always came each year, and the other was that if you licked your hand and pressed it on the birds on the wall-paper, they came off and you had a beautiful bird on your hand, but it didnt make up for the dissavantages of being there.

Maids Lav

The maids lav was about a hundred yards from the house across the yard, it was nicely tucked in between Nelly's kennel and the pullets pen and there was an evergreen hedge to shield the entrance from prying pullets eyes. The hedge was even more interesting than the maids lav, although I don't know what varity of greenery it was called, it had the great attraction of getting covered with catapillars every year, they were a creepy yellow, black and green kind, they must be a specialaty of that kind of bush because there was one by the drawing-room window and that suffered in the same way. They provided us with great amusement, and besides making them run races, and I'm sorry to say hanging them on gallows made of cotton and match sticks, we used to collect hundreds of the little creatures, put them in tins and shake them up and they used to hiss and hum, I can't think how they did this but its quite true, I do feel so sad for them when I think about it now.

To go back to the maids lav. it was built of brick and had rather a rotten door painted brown, on the roof was an enormouse open tank, Beatrix and I would climb up and put fish in, dace and geogens we had caught in the river, but we never saw them again because it was so deep, this tank wasn't used for sanitary purposes but supplied water to the horse trough, perhaps the fish got stuck in the pipe when the tap was turned on. The maids never grumbled about their lavatory, although we had some good ones with chains in the house, Daddy would have shot them if they had dared to use them so they never did even when it snowed, it wasn't even a two holer, just a rough piece of wood with a hole and bucket underneath. The walls were green distempered, beautifully decorated with snales, slugs and their tracks and a few sleepy spiders in the corners.

A man in the village used to empty the bucket, he had a key to the back gates and came at the dead of night, his name was Coddy Bennet. Chloe would stay awake the night he came his rounds, she said his cart had oil lamps hanging from it and smelt simply dreadful, and he would cry 'Muck, Muck, bring out your muck'. I'm glad he collected ours and we didn't have to take it out to him.

Walks

Our governess used to take us for a walk every day, Kathleen and Chloe went with their nursemaid Norah, sometimes I went with them but felt this was most undignified, that was the worst of coming in the middle of a large family, the older ones rather dispise you, and you dispise the babies of the family, also the governesses always wanted to push me onto Norah or who ever was nursemaid and they resented it and me.

We had the choice of about five suitable walks, there was the walk to Gorse station, Gorse was a pretty little village stiff with thatched cottages like old fashioned bee hives, there was a nice pub with a magpie and some strange hens kept in boxes, they had long white feathers like fur and were most attractive, meets were often held outside this pub, the hounds used to come by train, and we liked to watch them leaping out of the cattle truck, tongues out and tails waving, we did not hunt ourselves.

We called the walk to Barton the fairy way because there were so many blackthorn bushes all sparkling with blossom in the Spring, we used the nice twisty little path that followed the bends in the river, and there were many stiles shiney with use to climb over, parts of the path were of broken scattered flag stones, they always looked like peices of poached egg whites to me and I was quite surprised to find them hard to tread on. The governesses were rather fond of this walk because there were no hills to climb, only stiles, and they could sit on those. They didn't like taking us to Marlcliff much because we used to go mad when we got there and slide down the cliffs and ruin our knickers, we had to go through the dreadful roly poly field that was full of cows to get there.

Daddy used to take us to Two Waters, it was too far for the governesses, sometimes we would go by boat, there was a waterfall there and an old mill, Daddy used to use the mill for a shooting box at one time and a man called Monkeybrand used to look after it, he was great and hairy, once I found a large and beautiful spider with a lot of babies having a ride on its back, while I was looking at it, he came up behind me and suddenly put his great hand out and squashed them, they had looked so happy, but all that was left of them was a dark mess that smelt of ink, I always felt frit of him after that.

When we had Miss Grove for a governess, she had a sister who taught in St Stephen's Priors, so we used to go there nearly every day, it was a pretty village but had a damp closed in feeling, we had to go up and down a very steep hill called Marrage Hill to get there, we liked that because we could run down the hill very fast, also how ever much they mended and tarred the road little streams used to work their way out except in the dryist weather. There was an old man with a beard and side whiskers who used to sweep and mend the roads, his eyes were bright red because he got some lime in them once, he had a daughter called Hatty Houghton who was our cook, and a grand daughter called Olive with a thing called lupus or something on her nose, but it got better when she grew up.

A walk I hated was going to Shellford Siding, it smelt of cabbages and there were very ugly depressing houses with lots of shrubs round them, a man called Daddy Hill lived in one, he was a dwaf with a huge head, he used to come and play croquet with the grown ups and used a childs mallet, he was very kind but I couldn't bear to look at him. There was another awful thing in a field – just by the gate, a man had a billy goat that died and he buried it and left the horns sticking out of the grave, and they stayed like that for a long time, it was terrable.

Some Sad things to Do with Animals

We loved animals, but were sometimes unkind to insects and the lesser kind of reptiles, the poor ants forinstance, we would chase them with a magnifing glass in the sun and burn them, they used to frissel and pop poor little creatures, they smelt beastly too. Mary once burnt Daddy in the same way when he was asleep in a deck chair, he didn't stay asleep or smell the same as ants.

Another rather foul thing we did, but with the best intentions, was 'making worms better'. The worms with the joins in were the victims, we cut them in half on the old scar, a match stick or pine needle was inserted and the pieces were joined together and neatly bandaged with a blade of grass, we thought this strengthened them and made it much easier to burrow down in the soil when they were so nice and stiff, I feel full of remorse when I think of this now, how could they have turned corners or ever come up again all stiff like that. To make amends I always rescue those dried up worms you sometimes find on paths and put them some where damp and more suitable, so by now I must have saved far more worms than most people.

Catapillers came in for a certain amount of unkind treatment, squashing them to see what colour they were inside, we didn't do this much because they were always the same – green, we made rather nasty little swings for them and made them run races too.

We were kind to the dogs and loved them dearly, but Daddy was often beastly to them, kicking and throwing stones and always trying to poison Jimmy-the-Dog whom he hated, but Jimmy-the-Dog thrived on poison, he just sat under Granny's chair and growled a bit more, in the end he outlived Daddy. He wasn't so awful to the dogs when they were out for walks or even in the house, it was when they were in the garden he got so het up, really they did very little damage, the only damage they did was bite people who came to the back gates, he did sometimes have to buy errend boys new trousers, I always remember seeing the Old Doctor running in, purple in the face with Nelly hanging on his gaters, her teeth had got hooked in somehow and wouldn't come out.

Before I was old enough to look after the dogs Palmer used to, and they were frightfully neglected, poor dears, the shooting dogs were hardly ever let out all summer, their coats were all matted and eyes running, the kennels were filthy too, he was delighted when Nelly had to be shut up, sometimes she would have to stay in her kennel for nearly two months until one of the governesses took pity on her and let her out against Palmers orders. He hated all animals, he would chop Kitchners kittens heads off in the woodshed, and we could see blood all over the chopping block, other times he would drown them in a bucket, very slowly. Perhaps it was an inhibition that made him so cruil.

We had Kitchner for years and always thought she was a Tom, until she had kittens on Beatrix's bed one night, she kept having them all the time then, she went a very queer shape in time, but was a dear thing, even Daddy was quite fond of her, but when she was very old she developed astma and mange, instead of taking her to a vet Daddy shot her when she was asleep in the garden, he shot her from too close a range because he wanted to be sure she died at once, but it was awful and he wouldn't eat jam for ages after. Daddy was kind to the parrots and monkeys we had, even Jane the wicked one, Phillip the peacock loved him best of all, when Daddy died he just ran or rather flew away.

When Beatrix and I were about four, we did a frightful thing, we tried to ride the tame rabbits with the most drastic results, we had seen pictures of children riding rabbits and thought we could do the same, but we couldn't, and for years people said 'these are the children who squashed the rabbits'.

When the animals died, they received fine funerals, the procession was led by Beatrix's waggon as hearse, the poor little body was covered with flowers, we would all follow, dressed in anything immpressive we could find, when the body was buried Mary would read the burial service 'Ashes to ashes, dust, if God wont have you the Devel must'. Our marrage service was 'With this ring I thee wed and with this stick I clout thy head'. Once Beatrix and I had to be kind of bridesmaids with baskets of flowers, we were so disipointed when they didn't say it at all, at least the stick part, also they said the bridegroom would give us a brootch or something but that didn't happen either.

When we were about ten years old the barbers wife gave us a young Billy goat, Mammie said we were to take it back at once because of the smell, but we felt if someone had got to smell it why not us, so we thought the engine room would be a good place to hide it, it was difficult getting it up the steps and when it was there it kept bleating away but no one seemed to hear it. We fed it on bread and milk, it must have got very bored with its food and being shut up like that, after a few days it jumped out of the window, poor thing, anyway it wasn't hurt, some children found it and brought it back to the house, they told how they had seen it jumping from a window and we got into very great trouble, Mammie had her mouth boxed up for days afterwards, she always did this when she was cross because her teeth stuck out.

Education

When I was about five years old Granny said we were a disgrace, we needed licking into shape, so insted of the dead vicar's daughters who used to arrive on bycicles to teach us, they advertised in *The Times* for a strong disiplarian and the result was Miss Vann. She had always been in the best famlies before she came to us but she was rather on her last legs by the time we got her, that is if she had any legs, all the same she was still a strong disiplarian. I came in for the worst of it, perhaps because she always said I was spoilt or it may have been because I was the youngest in her charge. She quite liked Beatrix but was rather afraid of Mary who was ten when she first came to us. Kathleen and Chloe still had a nurse called Norah to look after them, Chloe was quite a small baby with rather a mauve face at this time.

During Miss Vann's reign I got a smacked bottom nearly every night in advance before she went down stairs for her dinner, that was in case I talked to Beatrix instead of going to sleep, it was a consolation to know I could talk as much as I liked without further punishment, but I used to dread having

46

my hair done in the mornings, it was curly and always full of tangles, if I moved my head an inch while she brushed it she would give me an awful crack with the back of the brush, it was almost worse for Beatrix who was the only one of us to have straight hair, Miss Vann used to curl it with rags into beastly things called kidneys that stuck in her head all night.

She was the only governess Granny didn't bully, I think she suspected quite wrongly that the others all were in love with Daddy, she would walk past their bedroom windows with heavy footsteps which she hoped sounded like Daddies, if the governesses looked out of the window to see what the queer noise was her worst suspicions were confirmed, in some cases they were only wearing their petticoats or camisoles, so their lives were made a misery until they had to leave, most of the governess left after a few weeks except Miss Vann and Miss Glide

Miss Vann was quite seventy, she wore black spectials and all her frocks had high necks strengthened by wire, the bodices had bumperty lace inserted, there were spots of egg stuck in the deep parts, I tried putting egg yoke in the deep parts of the smocking on my frocks, but got smacked again, so it must have been a mistake. She wore three pairs of knickers at night and five in the daytime, she had pneumonia while she was with us and the nurse told me about all these knickers, so it just shows the more clothes you wear the more pneumonia you get.

For three years Miss Vann stayed with us, the grown-ups had a great respect for her, but we hadn't, we rather hated her, poor thing, I guess she must have been longing to dose over the fire and have a little peace at her age, instead she had to live with six little hooligans who were pretty beastly to her. When we went to parties she pinned me to her dress most of the time and if I was offered another piece of cake or anything and she considered I'd had enough she would pinch me to let me know I was not to accept, if I did I got another pinch twice as bad. Then there came a day when she dragged me upstairs to put me to bed for a punishment, but when we reached the top of the stairs I suddenly thought I couldn't stand all these punishments any more and before I hardly knew what I'd done I'd kicked her down the stairs, she went down head first and landed with her head in a kind of brass pot that lived at the bottom, she looked so awful going down, like a broken old rag doll in her dark pink frock, then she lay quite still at the bottom so I thought now she is dead and my tummy felt all hollow, so I crawled away and hid under a bed, there was a lot of fluffy dust there and it got in my eyes, nose and throat, but when I cried it all came out again then I went to sleep. When they found me hours later no one was cross, I kept waiting for them to be, but they wern't, not even Miss Vann, there she was with a big broose like a horn sticking out of her forehead and she kept saying 'Oh dear, I hope I won't be disfigured for life'. She left soon after this, she said we were getting too old for her.

While she was with us we had meals in the morning-room because she said she wouldn't sit down to a table with anyone who swore so much as Daddy, it was rather dull in the morning-room and we were glad to go back to meals with the grown-ups after she departed. For a few weeks we had no one to look after us and our hair got matted and clothes got all torn and messed up, then Mammie washed all our heads and said it was disgusting she couldn't leave us a few days before we ruined our clothes and got scurf in our hair, she brushed our hair very hard and made a kind of shissing sound as she did it, then in the afternoon Miss Glide came and she stayed for years, Mammie and Daddy loved her and even we quite liked her, certainly there were not so many quarrels between the grown-ups while she was with us, she even managed the Granny Situation quite tacfully. She was the only really successful governess we had, she wasn't very good at teaching perhaps, but she tried to make the lessons interesting, she was the first governess who read to us in the evenings and seemed to enjoy taking us for walks and playing games with us, she was poplar in the village and was in great demand at tennis parties and dances. Eventually she left to get married to her Jack who was a farmer in Somerset, they had been engaged even before she came to us and she used to crotchet away at her trousseau in every spare moment.

After she left the grown-ups decided to send Mary to Malvern girls college, there was an awful fuss getting her clothes ready, Daddy didn't like the idea of her going much but Mammie wanted her to be like our Hillersdon cousins who were all at large boarding schools. When all the preparations were finished, off Mary went looking pretty green and Mammie departed for a few days rest at Hillersdon but she was soon summonsed back by a telegram saying Mary had run away from school and they couldn't trace her. The next day she was discovered eating buns on a station and Daddy brought her home again, Mammie was simply fourious but Daddy was in the position of saying 'I told you so' and made a great fuss of Mary when she came home. The school refused to have her back

49

which upset Mammie still more, In the end she was sent to a much smaller school with Beatrix as her companion, neither of them liked it very much but they didn't attempt to run away.

I was left at home with Kathleen and Chloe as companions, at first I didn't like the idea of being classed with the younger ones and I missed Beatrix, though later I enjoyed being the eldest at home, I stayed downstairs for dinner with the grown-ups and I expect grew rather spoilt and bossy. A few rather feeble women came they were called nursery governesses which meant they were expected to do all Norah's work and teach us as well (Norah had left to get married too) none of these unfortunate women stayed long, then we had a term or two at Miss Goaty Morgan's school after that we did no more lessons for a year or two and devoted our time to measles, whooping cough and chickenpox.

When I was twelve Mary left school and I went in her place, I hated it and cant bear to think of it even now. Those awful bells and all the discomforts, tepid bath water foul stoves, we didn't see an open fire for months on end, then there was the disgusting food, slimy boiled suet puddings with big lumps of fat in them, burnt porrage, bread and margerene and all the other boiled watery messes we had, how I longed for fresh fruit and to see a really beautiful face, The mistresses were all plain with lumpy figures and blotchy faces, the girls were not so bad but they looked a bit like the food we eat and we had to wear hideous gym frocks and rather dirty flannel blouses, you were considered vain if you took the slightest interest in your appearance, my shoulder leangth curly hair had to be dragged back by a black ribbon and a beastly little fussy tail stuck out behind. You were thought frightful if you said you would like to get married when you were grown up, you had to say you would like to be a games mistress or something dull like that, for a time I said I was going to nurse lepers because that sounded more interesting and no one could say I was looking for a husband in a leper colony, then I got rather frit I might be taken seriously and would find myself in a leper colony before I knew quite where I was.

To my family games were a nightmare too, none of us were any good at them, I never scored a goal at hockey all the time I was at school, even in the practice on the lawn, usually during hockey I would shut my eyes and count sixty slowly, when I had repeated this sixty times an hour had passed and the beastly game was over for the afternoon. Tennis wasn't quite so bad but the grown-ups supplied us with enormouse flat ended racquets weighing about twenty six oz left over from Daddies youth, we were awfully ashamed of them and they were so heavy to lift it more than spoilt our game.

We were surprised to find the girls quite liked us although they said we were a bit mad, on the whole they were fairly nice to us and we always had partners for our crocidile walks and were not teased too much, some of the girls had a pretty foul time, schools seem to be very snobish places, the ones who had rich or titled parents had a much better time than the ones who were shabby or came from small suburban homes, very plain girls too were treated like dirt, fortunately for we were presumably wealthy as we took all the extras and had a fairly large country home, all the same we never dar'd to ask anyone home for the holidays, they might have thought us madder than they did already if we had, there were other reasons too.

Coming home was rather disipointing, we looked forward to our return so much, then everything fell dreadfully flat. Mammie seemed rather bored by the fact we were home again, Mary was frankly hostile, I believe Daddy was quite pleased to see us, for the first few days anyway, he always drove to meet us with Wilkes, and on the drive home told us all the village and garden news. Mammie would have been more glad to see us if we had been more of a credit, I think. We never won a prize or shon in any way and must have been a great disipointment to her, as it was they hardly ever even opened our reports, considering all the money they spent on our education they took remarkably little interest in it, and never came to the sports or to visit us during term time

Black Monday

About once a month Daddy went to Birmingham on business, it was always on a Monday when he went and there couldn't have been more fuss if he had been going to the ends of the earth. The evening before Wilks was ordered for nine o'clock unless it was very fine, in this case he would walk the two miles to the station through the fields, but Wilks always brought him home in the evening. On these fatal Mondays he used to get up at six and there wasn't much peace unless everyone got up at the same time which was a bit grim in the winter, it took him three hours to eat his breakfast and get dressed and most important of all find a suitable buttonhole.

His favourate clothes were britches and the shinest pair of leggins in the world, he polished these and his shoes himself, because he loved shoes so much and had a room lined with shelves all filled with beautiful shiney shoes, boots and white buckskin boots, he spent hours looking after them. With the britches he wore a very light gray Norfolk jacket and coat and cap to match all of extremely thick tweed. If he had to attend a board meeting he wore something rather darker but he much prefired very light things, maybe because he was so dark, he was a very vain man.

Unless he cut a rose for his buttonhole he liked to wear something out of season, the more out of season the better, so there was a great comb out of the greenhouses to find a suitable bloom that would raise envy in his business aquaintance's hearts, sometimes he would take a pear, peach or particularly fine apple, he wouldn't have needed much encouragement to take a marrow along with him, but I don't remember him doing so.

When he was at last ready, with his silver flask filled with brandy in case he was overcome by the journey, we all had to flock to the door to see him off, and until the carriage had dis-apeared from sight we had to say Good Luck, Good Luck and then go on saying more Good Lucks. Once I wouldn't say good Luck at all, just went on eating my toast and marmalaid, the grown-ups Granny in particular were horrorfied and I was smacked and locked in the bootroom, usually when I was locked up in there I used to eat the galoches, but this time it was too soon after breakfast so I cried until I was sick, they had to let me out after that.

As soon as Daddy went out of the house things started to go wrong somehow, Mammie would sometimes get all fierce about cleaning the billardroom and make all the maids cross or get some awful new idea that the dogs were never to come in the house again or she would borrow our paints, copy a very shakey picture of a Madonna and child and say she would have been a great artist if it hadn't been for all us children. Sometimes she would say she felt very poorley and sit over the morning-room fire biting the skin off oranges, it was better when she was like this, and we would find the oranges stuffed behind cushions afterwards and eat them.

Granny always worked up rather a grudge against Daddy when he was away, chiefly because he took the keys of the wine cellar with him, also the governess's had some of her grudge. They kept out of her way as much as possible but couldn't excape her at lunch time, so she used to have a kind of governess baiting then. The well established ones could hold their own fairly well but the timid new ones fell like ninepins, it was fasanating yet frightening to watch her at it. Mary carried on the Monday governess baiting after Granny died, but she wasn't so clever as Granny so it was all rather boring from our point of view.

Some Mondays Granny worked Mammie up against Daddy or if she failed in this or was reproved for her treatment of the governesses they quarreled between themselves and grew fiercer and fiercer as the day went on, Mammie would tear her hankies to shreds and Grannie gave hysterical screaming laughs at frequent intervals. It usually reached a climax at about six o'clock and Granny would retire to her room to pack her boxes and shouting downstairs, 'Send for Wilks, I will have Wilks' Everyone knew Wilks was already on his way to the station to meet Daddy, all the same the maids would carry down her great black ark shaped trunks laughing and winking at each other as they struggled with the great things, and would leave them grouped round the front door with Granny sitting in their midst, her jaw trembling with anger all dressed in black vails, plumes and camphor sented sealskins, there she sat, the centre of the stage all set for Daddies arrival. It rather depended on the kind of day he had had and how much he wanted his dinner, if he was hungry and things had gone badly he would tell her to 'damn-well-go-and-lets-have-some-peace-in-the-house', this led to more trouble and comotion and it would be hours before it calmed down, fortunately he usually gave her a stiff whiskey and fussed her up a bit and it all passed over, the maids would drag the trunks up the stairs again, not laughing any more and there was rather a feeling of general anticlimax about the house.

The River that ran past our door

We spent most of our days playing in or on the river, its a wonderful thing to happen to you when you are a child, to have a river running past your door, or when you are grown-up for that matter. The wier was only a few yards beyond our house so the water flowed fast, we could always hear the noise of rushing, falling water. When the floods came in the Spring the noise was terrific, I always knew when the floods had come because of the rushing sound, even before it was light the seagulls would be crying and men would be shouting, and as soon as the darkness started to lift I would dress and hurry into the garden to see how far the water had come, I usually found some of the others there and we would watch the different kind of things that went floating rapidly past, hens in hen houses clucking away, pigs screaming and making their throats all red where they had scraped it with their short struggling legs, empty boats, barrels of beer and masses of loose timber, it all went sailing past. For miles all you could see was shimmering water, trees and an occaisonal hedge. Men would be trying to rescue their horses and cows from boats with ropes, they usually succeeded, but the sheep didn't have much chance.

When we were very young people would sometimes forbid us to play on the path that ran by the river, but it didn't make any difference, we always did. We used to fall in but were never completely drowned, the village children often were though. There was a family called Drinkwater and no less than five of them were drowned, they were a very poor family, the mother was very handsome and fierce looking, with a figure rather like a withie, which was quite suitable because she stripped the withies on the river bank as her living, most of the village women did and after they were stripped they were made into baskets and cradels. The trippers were always getting drowned but it didn't matter much, the village was glad to have the money they brought but were tierd of the noise and illegitamate babies with quite untraceable fathers.

One winter, the only time I remember it happening, the river froze completely except for two rather frightening holes near the weir. I would stand on the edge and think how frightful it would be if my feet just slipped a few inches and I fell in and was carried away under the ice, much worse than ordinary drowning, my head would go bump, bump under the ice until I was sucked below to be tightly clasped by the clutching weeds. One day as we were doing our lessons in the cottage overhanging the river, we heard a strange creaking and a hammering sound, then there was a clatter and a horse and cart went driving past, driven by an old man who was a cripple because he fell off a house once. We stopped doing our lessons and ran onto the ice too, but we couldn't overtake the horse and cart. Daddy put on his skates and joined us, so we did no more lessons that morning. Mammie who had seen the horse and cart also started to scream as soon as she discovered her family on the ice too, she tore up and down the river bank dragging a ladder which is supposed to be of use to drowning people, presumably to walk up from the river bed on. Sometimes she would drop the ladder and wring her hands in anguish, she was a great wringer of hands, eventualy all this oppersition got too much for us and we sadly left the ice. After a few days it started to thore rapidly, when it got to the stage of having about six inches of water above the surface, mammie suddenly got all enthusiastic and insisted that we were all cowards and must learn to skate, we had no skates but that was a minor detale, Palmer was ordered to drag Kathleen and Chloe on a sledge and there was an awful row when he refused, it ended in both Mammie and Granny packing their boxes because they couldn't continue to live under the same roof as cowards and insobordinate servants. Of course they didn't realy go, it was one of those Black Mondays when Daddy was away.

Courious Habits of Bats, Moths and Earwigs

The maids said if a bat got in our hair it would flutter, flutter and make such a fussywussy mess of our hair it would have to be all shorn off before you could get the bat out again. Apparently hundreds of their friends had had bats in their hair, always with fatal results, bats seemed to spend the entire night trying to find long haired girls they could get all tangled up with, on the other hand earwigs spent the day and sometimes night finding ears to creep into, with intent to make the earowners go deaf for life or raving mad. Then bats got in belfrys too, so these two loathsome creatures caused havoc as far as I could see

Our sweep got an earwig in his ear and went quite deaf in one ear, but after about ten years it suddenly woke up (it was Spring) and came running out of his ear and never returned as far as I have heard, so the sweep could hear perfectly again and grew quite fameous, they said there were more affaliation orders against him than any other man in the village, but that may have been because he used to arrive so early in the morning.

I always slept with my hair tied under my chin as a protection against both these pests, it didn't look very inviting for bats, all tied like that, and kept my ears well covered, but it was frightfully hot and scratchy in summer.

Some nights we would wake to the awful plopping noise of bats flipping around our bedrooms, we would cry BAT, BAT, and anyone who heard was in honour bound to come to our rescue with pillows, tennis racquets or any other suitable impliment for shooing bats away, we dared not light a candle because we were so afraid of the bats seeing our hair, and it was all rather frightening rather like a witches sabbath. When Kathleen and Chloe felt lonely or had a nightmare they would cry 'Bat, O a Bat', and when we loyally dashed to their bedroom they proved to be quite batless so we came to an agreement that unless they said Batx we wouldn't bother to help them. An x at the end of any word ment it was extra true, and no one dared lie with an x in case God struck them dumb.

Beatrix was frit to death of moths and almost had hysterics when she discovered them in her room, Chloe and I would catch them for her on condition she gave us a Minto (she always had a store of sweets and chocolate in her neat drawers) Sometimes when we were hungry we would catch moths and put them in her bedroom on our way to bed. Beatrix really had good reason to be afraid of them, before the resrecton she hardly noticed the things, but even now after all these years she is as frit as she was that summer evening we found those dead moths in the attic. They were a kind called Bobhowlers and were about as large as sparrows, we usually found them in the boat house and this was the first time we had seen any dead so we held them near the candle to examine them better. Then to our horror they began to come alive, first their horried little trunks unfurled, gradualy their eyes all lit up and became bright red all glowing, then their furry bodies started to twitch and their wings to shiver but they never became completely alive, not alive enough to walk or fly, the glowing ruby eyes was the worst part of it. We hated them so much but something unhealthy compelled us to spend most of the night reserecting these dead moths, we felt kind of powerful, like God, but it was disipointing that as soon as we took them away from the candles rays they collapsed again. Eventually we went to bed and the next morning I just sicked and sicked till I'd got all the horror out of me, but Beatrix didn't.

Dinner Parties

Mammy adored giving dinner parties, she prepared most of the food herself, she was an excellent cook, and spared not trouble or expense. The morning before a dinner party was spent in the kitchen, she wore a huge white linen apron and made a great mess, I've never seen any one dirty more utencils in such a short time, the older maids lost their tempers and the younger ones their wits, still it was nice in the kitchen, there was a good smell and I would beat up the whites of eggs and lick the bowls. A great deal of time was spent over the diningroom table too, but I wasn't allowed to help, because my hands took the shine off the silver and glass, and I couldn't help stealing the desert, there were candle sticks with branches coming out of them, I liked to see them all lit just before the dinner party started. Once Mammy felt so exhausted with all her preperations that she drank too much sherry an hour or two before people were due to arrive, it was rather awful, Palmer had to be sent to fetch Daddy who was out somewhere, and all the guests had to be put off till the next evening, they said Mammy was indisposed and she was.

When there were dinner parties Palmer was put into tails, rather too large they were, then he was butler for the evening, he rather liked it. As soon as the visitors started to arrive we got out of bed and sat on the front stairs, sometimes we tied black cotten all across the landing, so that they got all tied when they went to the lav after dinner, we didn't if they let us have marangues. If we saw any going into the diningroom we would shout WE WANT MARANGUES, the maids would tell us to shut up, but we knew if we went on long enough Daddy would hear and bring us up marangues and small fondant sweets made like babies in cradles, sometimes we would get into the diningroom itself, Mammy didn't like it when we did because we had got rather dirty and some of our nighties lost by this time. Other times we would sit in the kitchen and devour odds and ends as they came out of the diningroom, and listen to Palmer telling the cook what had been going on, he was always disgusted to see the way the respectable village matrons dressed in the evenings. One dinner party was rather ruined because Ermentrude the pig choose to bring forth her young the very same evening, and Palmer had to divide the evening between the pig sty and diningroom, she had fourteen.

Things fell rather flat after people had finished eating, Mammy was very good at feeding people but she didn't know how to entertain and being deaf made complications. If Daddy got the chance he liked to take all the men to the billard room, the poor women were banished with the port, and would sit in the drawingroom waiting for the men to come and they never did. If the men had been well primed by their wives they refused to play billards, then there would be music, Beatrix would play the violin, when she was older, she was the only one of us who performed, she was at 'Down in the Forest' stage, Daddy would sing 'Van Tromp was an Admeral' and 'Will of the Whisp', he had the loudest, flatest voice there ever was, the reigning governess usually played the piano, occaisionally the visitors were allowed to do something too.

Punishments

Our most usual punishment was being shut up in the boot-room, at least that was what Mammie did with us, at first I would cry because that was the proper thing to do, really I didn't mind being in there very much, after I was tierd of crying there were always the galoshers to eat holes in, I liked eating rubber, my inderrubbers never lasted me more than a week, when I had eaten several toes away I would tie all the laces into knots, there were quite a lot of things like that you could do in there, Daddy didn't like us being put in there much. It was different for Beatrix, she had a thing she now calls claustophibia, if you have it you hate being shut up and scream and get violent if you are, once while she was in there she broke the glass panels of the door and threw the glass at Mammie, there was a lot of blood and screaming and she was never put in there any more. Then I discovered I could climb out of the tiny window, it took me three years to think of that, then our leather smelling prison was abandoned. Mammie tried smacking us, but she wasn't much good at it, she couldnt aim straight somehow, anyway we could hit harder than she could and bite too. She used to box her mouth up when she was in a temper, it was difficult for her because her teeth were the sticking out kind, when ever we saw her with her mouth like this we knew she was on 'the ramp' she would start off by saying 'we were just like your father' and end by saying 'you shall have no jam for tea' that always made us laugh, we didn't like jam much anyway, and we knew she would have forgotten all about it in another five minutes, in any case she seldom had tea with us in those days and if she had we would have just eaten cake and honey.

Granny in a temper was pretty grim, her jaw would tremble and she would give screeching laughs and say frightening things about cursing us and that we would shrivel in Hell and that our soals would scream in the pine trees at night, then she would say we were no better than Street Arabs and Charity Winks and should be horsewhipped, once Daddy took her at her word and did horsewhip me, it was so dreadful I couldn't even cry out, then Granny got frit and kept shouting, 'No more, you will kill the child, stop, stop' it seemed as if he had got so worked up he would never stop, but when he did it was even more painful, that was the worst beating he ever gave me, it was on Primrose Day too, my crime was I'd got a finger of bread stuck in my egg at breakfast, in trying to get it out the wretched egg seemed to fly up and broke on the wall, it made rather an unsightly mess on the wall but was nothing compared to the mess I was in when he had finished with me. I kept having a frightful nightmare that Daddy was a bellowing bull chaising me round the ash tree for nights after.

Daddy was very fierse with us, we would suddenly hear an

angry trumpeting noise and he would grab as many of us as he could and bang our heads together, I got the most beatings, Kathleen and Chloe hardly any because he had grown rather tame by the time they were old enough to be naughty.

Once when Beatrix was a baby he got so furious because of her crying he threw her down the stairs, fortunatly a cook called Harriat caught her at the bottom and saved her life, after that Harriat kept her in her bedroom at night so that he couldn't hear her crying which was a good thing in case there hadn't been anyone to catch her the next time, but Harriat had to leave soon after because her feet smelt.

Boats and Fishing

When we were rather small we were not supposed to play on the path that ran on the banks of the river, of course we always did and no one seemed to notice, when the floods came we would walk along the path on our stilts splashing through the water. Palmer had made the stilts, they were quite good ones, except mine were rather bow legged, I dont know if I made them get like that, or if they made my legs bend, but I noticed that my legs got a bit bow at that time and they still are.

We got more happiness from the river than anything. We all learnt how to row in a big flat bottomed boat and by the time I was six I could row in the ordinary rowing boat, we never had a skif but could go quite fast in the canoe if we used the double paddles. Mammy hardly ever went on the river, when she did she would put on a special 'river frock' and large floppy hat. Once a year we hired a green punt, it was simply enormous, it was usually used to carry the withies, Mammy called it the 'Superb' All the family – including Granny – who was all covered in vales and plumed hats, and a feather boa, used to go for a river picnic in this, Palmer standing at the back had to get the boat along somehow with one oar, Daddy worked the old fashioned gramophone with its green horn. Granny sat high up on the food hamper and wasps would keep getting in her vale, she quarreled with the governess most of the time when she wasn't slashing at the wasps.

Mammy would spend hours preparing the food for picnics, we had lovely things like salmon mainaise, oyster patties, marangues and strawberries or rasberries and cream, there was cider to drink, even Granny enjoyed the food. Sometimes our batty camera cousin would come and take snapshots of us all, rather awful ones.

Although we played by or on the river most of the time, we were not much good at swimming, Mary and Beatrix were fairly good, but I used to be so frightened when I got out of my depth, I felt witchs hands scratching and trying to catch my legs, perhaps it was only the weeds. Kathleen started to develope a figure rather early and she grew so shy she wouldn't bathe any more, Chloe was just terrified because Mary used to drag her in and duck her, Daddy said the first one to swim the river – across not along – could have a pound, Beatrix won it, I did manage to swim across the river in the end, but Daddy was dead then.

In the hay making season they used to let most of the water out of the river so that loads of hay could cross at the fords, then we would dig about in the muddy bed of the river and hope to find treasures, it smelt rather.

Kathleen and I were mad about fishing, we would lie on our tummies on the floating landingstage and gaze into the clear water, we would put a small piece of bread in, at first just minnows would come, then geodgeon, soon there would be hundreds all fighting over the piece of bread, we would lower our hooks baited with a worm among the seething fish and up one would come, we just used string not fishing rods, we liked to feel the tugging of the fish with our hands and the first nibbles. Sometimes we caught as many as fifty in a day, in the evening we would throw them back, they were a lighter colour than the other fish when we first put them back. There was a floating boathouse, rather like an ark with boats coming out instead of animals, under the boat house was the best place to catch perch, they liked the shade, perch were my favourate fish, I always called them the loardly ones, they looked so grand with their stripes and red fins, like tigers, all the smaller fish would scurry away as they aproached. Sometimes we would catch prickerly fish with big heads, they were called Daddy roughs, I haven't met any since. We would catch roach by the wier, but you had to use a proper rod and line, and you couldn't see them before you caught them. Palmer showed me how to catch eels with a night line, they were almost impossible to unhook, usually I just cut the line, they looked funny with a piece sticking out, as if they were smoking a pipe, I kept them covered or they excaped like snakes, then I found they disapeared even when I kept them covered, soon I discovered Palmer took them as bate for pike, that was why he had taught me how to catch them, so I gave up after that, they were so slimy, too. When the village people saw a dead goat or pig floating in the river looking pretty old, they would draw it onto the bank and all eels would come squirming out, they would take them home and stew them for supper, we didn't, but we did something nearly as bad, we would hit their swollen bellys with a boat hook and paddle away as fast as possible to excape the spout to putred smelling water that shot up in a castrade. Daddy was once fishing quiertly in a boat, after a time he could hear something bumping about a bit under the boat, when he moved away, there was a very dead boy floating about, it was one of the Drinkwaters.

The Other Side of the River

The opersite side of the river to our garden was The Big Meadow, a large field, shared by most of the village, they each had a cow or horse grasing in it so it was rather a mix up There was always something going on in the Big Meadow, either someone trying to catch a horse, cavervans arriveing or a fishing contest being held, there was one old man who fished there every day, except in the very depts of winter, we called him 'the Old Geeser' then he ceased to come and we heard he was dead, there he had been every time I looked out of our school room window, it took a long time to get used to the landscape without him, even now when I try to remember things like the date of the War of the Roses or seven nines I see this rather tubby dark little figure squatting on the river bank.

For a time in the spring the field would become empty, and we had to keep to the paths when we walked through, but we did not mind because we knew it was the prelude to hay-making, then we would take our tea over in boats, the newly cut hay in its foaming rows seemed as good as the sea to us, no one seemed to mind when we made nests and houses in it, we had rides on the hay wagon, but there was one thing that made me sad, there were quantaties of poor frogs with their legs mutilated by the mower, and some were cut right in half. One morning we were excused our lessons and allowed to play in the hay, but when we returned we discovered Dash the old black and white spanial was dead, he had been shot while we had played, poor Dash, he was too old for Daddy to take shooting any more so he had been shot himself, it seemed an ungrateful and unimaginative thing to do to the poor dog, we all missed him so much they brought us a white mongeral puppy with a face like a fox, she was called Nelly and had numerous puppies.

About twice a year they had a fair in the Big Meadow or the little field next to it, we always went every day it lasted unless we had measles, Daddy and Mammy loved the fairs almost as much as we did, I think I would rather hear roundabout music than any symphony concert, I know Beatrix would be disgusted to hear me say so, but its so gladsad somehow and makes me feel brave, late at night long after we were in bed we could hear the music floating over the river, and see the reflected moving lights on our walls, it was beautiful to lie in bed like that.

Some nights we would wake to hear strange shouts coming from the Big Meadow 'Come now Blossom, steady old Bess, Coup Coup' then we would hear horses hoves, we would look out of the windows and there were men with lanterns trying to catch the horses, it took them a very long time, the sky would be all lit up and somewhere there would be a haystack or cottage on fire, often by the time the horses were caught and harnessed to the fire engine the glow had almost departed from the sky.

The Trippers

Awful people called Trippers used to come to our village on Public Holidays in the Summer, they would arrive in shoals from the nearest station, the river was the attraction. They hired boats from Hollands and on the river they went, but they often ended in it. They couldn't row or punt, but splashed, screamed, showed their braces and got drunk, they sweated and got sick and fell in the river, we didn't help them out with a boat hook, we just hoped they would drown, sometimes they did. Mary once found a fat, redfaced man hanging on our landing-stage, he said 'For Gods sake help me kid' but she hit him with a paddel and he had to let go, some one elce came and saved him in a boat, this was a good thing really or she might have been a murderess or perhaps she would have got off with manslaughter.

Maybe we were rather hard on the trippers, but they really were beastly and were always giving the village girls babies and making an awful noise, the babies as well as the trippers.

Dish face

The Old Doctors' wife said my face was the shape of a dish –
a dish the wrong way round, I looked in the mirror and it was,
just like the breakfast dish of bacon and eggs that appeared
most mornings. I couldn't bear to look at it any more, my face
or the dish. I still feel shy of the shape of my face although its
altered now.

Click

Two of my back teeth grew great holes, all black, they didnt hurt much the holes. Mary and Beatrix had recently paid rather a lot of visits to the dentest, and there had been rows about bills, so nothing was done about my teeth with their caverns, sometimes at night I worried if the holes would spread till I was all hole, but they didn't, then I found it was rather nice to suck them, it made rather an amusing noise, a long drawn *click*, at first I did it when I was alone in the garden, then I found it was more satisfactory after meals, all bits of meat and stuff came out, other people did not like this at all, when I made those *clicking* noises, they said it was simply disgusting, I didn't believe them and continued to do so. Then one afternoon I was alone on the river in the canoe, I went slowly past Hollands' Pleasure Gardens, watching the people having refreshments at the green tables, I envied the ones drinking pop, then I noticed a large woman in black, with an enormouse hat and high laced boots, she was all alone, I watched her finish her ham tea with relish, she laid down her knife and fork and gaised into space, then she started sucking her teeth, terriffic lingering sucks that ecoed and vibrated accross the river, I listened, fasinated and disgusted, no wonder she was alone, did I really sound like that? Quickly I paddled away from that disturbing sound, never any more did I suck my teeth.

Dolls and Games of Distruction

Charles trousers were just two stripey cotton tubes really but his jacket covered this dificiency, and you wouldnt have known they wern't real trousers unless you had a debunking eye, Mary had, and exposed him the very first time she saw him, 'Those arn't proper trousers' she said 'they don't cover his bottom, anyway he's only a girl doll with its hair cut short' I tried to explain if that was true all toys were girls because none of them were really like boys, but she just said I was rude. All the same Chloe and I still loved and played with Charles, he had a friend called Belinda, who was rather beautiful, and had jointed thumbs, we made her a yellow wig out of the drawing-room mat when we had brushed her original head of hair away. Chloe and I played with Charles and Belinda every day for years, except when Mary and Beatrix were home from school, I didn't like them to know I was still at the doll stage, I tried to pretend I liked tennis, poetry and religeon too.

We three who were left at home dreaded the hollidays,

Mary was so patronising when she came home, 'well kids, you havn't grown much' or 'Barbara where did you get that red frock, I told you nobody but me is allowed to wear red in this house, you have damn well got to take it off at once' so off it came and my red hair ribbon too. Beatrix wasn't so bad, we shared the same bedroom and the first night home she used to take a bag of biscuits, oranges, chocolate powder and anything elce like condenced milk to bed with her, she said she was starved at school, sometimes she was sick.

Another kind of doll game we used to play was 'match-sticks' we used to collect fallen flower petals and dress the match sticks in them, a daisy made a fine hat, a dandilion was a Queens crown, a rose petal made a good frock tied in place with a blade of grass, and perhaps a smaller petal for an apron, snapdragons made super frocks with a back and front, but they always had to be maids frocks, they had white peoney petals as nightdresses, wallnut shells were their beds, it was rather a good game to play by yourself.

Quite suddenly Chloe and I got a craze for throwing per-fectly good things away, it started in the holidays when our other games were rather surpressed. It was always Chloes' things that were distroyed, we would burn her books slowly, page by page, break her dolls heads off and distroy toys she was really fond of, an awful gleam would come in our eyes and we would tear a teddy bears head off, burn it, then throw the body in the river. Then we started on clothes, we would hurridly burn a pair of her socks in the morning-room fire, or rip a hanky to shreds, one morning feeling rather ambitious we tied several of her nightdresses to a brick and threw them in the river, they must have come undone or something because Mary found out, there was such a row we gave up our life of distruction, partly because there was nothing much left of Chloes to distroy.

Mice and Owls

When Kathleen was twelve, she went all owl, I don't know what caused it, maybe some one said she looked like one, she did rather, with her big dark eyes, small face and sticking out ears, anyway she just went owl crazy. At dusk she would go into the garden and screetch to the owls and they screetched back in answer, often she stayed out long after dark making wierd, frightening noises. During the day she sat doseing in a tree, it must have been at a time when we were governessless, because she didn't come down for lessons and often not for meals, noone said anything about it though. Although owls eat mice, Kathleen didn't, on the contrary, she shared with Chloe about a hundred pibald and white mice, they kept them in a large meatsafe in the yard, it smelt horried when you passed, but the dogs and cats thought it a lovely smell, and sat around, licking their chops, waiting for one to excape, this happened quite frequently so they did not wait in vain. Each morning Kathleen had a rollcall and if any mouse was missing she sat in the ashtree crying and sobbing as loud as she could, really rather enjoying herself. We got sick to death of waking up each morning to Kathleens woe, and often threatened to let the whole lot loose, they wern't very nice mice in any case, they got kind of degenerate, all living in such cramped quarters and being so closely related, they were descended from a pair we had had given us some years before. We sold some at a village fete once for 1/- each which was a good price, but it had to go to charity, we handed them to our customers in paper bags, some excaped and caused confusion, people do fuss so about mice, so our stall was closed and merchantdice returned home in disgrace.

After Chloe developed rhumatic fever, and was an invalede for such a long time, Kathleen forgot about owls, but there was stiil some trouble over the mice. She started to attend a small school that was started in the village and seemed to be fairly happy there, she was the eldest, at home she was the youngest but one and much the smallest, beastly people would say 'fancy letting your younger sister grow so much taller than you' and 'Chloe is such a beautiful girl and Kathleen such an odd little thing, very backward too I believe' I don't think people say such stuped things in front of children these days.

Engin Room

The engine house backed on to the coach house, it was quite large, about as big as an ordinary house, downstairs was the engine that pumped the water in some misterious way from the river, when there were floods the water was all brown and muddy but there wern't any fish in it, our drinking water sometimes had newts that came wissing out of the pump, so the old Doctor said we must have a filter, so we did but the maids wouldn't use it, it was luckey Palmer didn't feel like that about the engine or we would have no water. He was the only person who knew how to work it, and when he was ill and on what he called 'the box' we just had to manage on what we could get out of the pump. There was a large loft above the engine room, you had to climb up a ladder to get there but it was very nice when you did, almost like a real room with a window and everything only it was rather a pity there were two wooden things for the belt to run through. When we first discovered this room it was stiff with old junk, lots of wierd books about religion and how to distinguish different kinds of drunkness, I should have thought people were drunk, very drunk or dead drunk but this isnt the case at all there are pages of different drunks, there were also a number of out of date magazenes which were rather more interesting. Then there were some fine bits of old furniture, chairs with three legs, the ends of brass bedsteads, enormouse mirrors decorated with fretsaw work, I think they were meant to go over mantlepieces and a turkish bath, we were rather shy of the turkish bath, it looked kind of rude and sordid, there was an oilstove too, which we used to cook chestnuts on. The grown-ups could never manage the steps so it was very private and Beatrix and I soon adopted it as our own playroom. We put a mat on the floor and arranged the best bits of furniture covering the worst junk with an old curtain, but it never looked like a real room, always 'rather engine room' even now if I find myself in rather a makeshift kind of house it reminds me of the engine room. We had a very large dollshouse and somehow we pusuaded Palmer to carry it up and there it stayed for years, it was Beatrix and my favourate plaything and kept us happy untill we were well into our teens.

The window looked out onto the village street and we liked to hang out and watch people, one evening we were talking to a girl we knew called Nora Humble, she used to come to our tennis parties, suddenly we heard the most blood curdling swears coming up the steps and through the door, observesly Daddy gone crackers about something, the girl below look so horrorfied but we just pretended it was nothing to do with us and went on talking, she said a frit goodnight and hurried off on her bycicle, not daring to climb out of the window we had to go down and face Daddies wrath, things like that were always happening.

Blackeye

They started a picture house at Swan Village, it was rather a tough kind of place, but sometimes Wilkes would drive us there to see Wild West films, there was a continuing one about a man called Elmo The Mighty, it went on for months and it didn't matter much if you missed a few installments, the grown-ups never went, but we loved to go. On the drive home, I would sit in the dark dreaming that I was being rescued by Elmo or perhaps it was Elmer, he was dark and handsome, but rather spoilt by a very hairy chest he was always showing it off which was a pity, I had to shut my eyes when it appeared.

One evening we elder ones returned rather late after a visit to the cinema, we were all in a kind of coma, degesting the film we had just seen, but we were soon rudely awakened, there was an awfull uproar, Mammy was screaming and crying in the morning-room, and Daddy bellowing away like a bull, as we came into the room he hurried out without speaking to us, he locked himself in the billiard-room, always his stronghold during rows. Mammy was in the most frightful state, it was difficult to make out what had happened, she seemed almost crazy, my heart sank and I felt all sick, the grown-ups always seemed to get rather beastly when they were by themselves. It appeared they had had one of their appauling rows and Daddy had locked her in their bedroom, in a way they almost enjoyed their anger, Mammy would deliberately work herself up into hysterics. In this case instead of walking out of her bedroom through the dressing-room door which wasn't locked, she jumped out of the window, I can't think why she didn't just stay in her room out of Daddy's way, but suppose she thought this an anticlimax, anyway she jumped out, it was a high window to fall from, luckely there was a verandah below and her fall was broken by this, but she was badly broozed and shocked by her excape, but she picked herself up from the gravel path and staggered into the house to continue her arguement with Daddy, when he saw she was loose again he beat her up and smacked her face, he was just getting ready to do it again when we came in, her face certainly looked in an awfull mess, but we didn't really feel sorry for her, only disgusted with them both, Granny was wailing over her, so we left them together and went to bed, but I felt so frightened my teeth would keep chattering. Eventually in spite of my chattering teeth I fell asleep, and awoke late the next morning, there were shimmering lights dancing on the walls caused by the sun shining on the river, so I felt happy and quite forgot the events of the previous evening, the gong boomed through the house before I was dressed, I hurried downstairs to find I was the last of us children to come down, the grown-ups were always late for breakfast. There was Mary spreading butter on her toast, her face looked yellow too, her long black hair hung all about her, it was lank and greasy and I wished she would plait it or do it up or something, Beatrix was at the silver bacon dish, the one I thought looked like my face, she was picking all the pink bits out and leaving the fat, Kathleen and Chloe were choking down their toast and honey, their governess Miss Smith would be here in a minute, Chloe put a big dab of honey in the middle of Granny's chair and grinned at Kathleen I was just making up my mind about bacon fat or limp toast, when there was a rattle at the door and Mammy came in very slowly, and all the horror of last night came back, although her face was very heavily coated in snow white powder, you could see it was all blotchy and bloated, but the frightful thing was her eye, it was completely enclosed in black and purple flesh, it showed up so dreadfully against the white powder, she walked right round the table, looking at each of us in turn, not saying anything at all, she wore a white jumper with short sleeves, her arms were all broused too, but it was her eye that was so dreadful. I ran from the room, the engin-room was the only place I thought would be safe from that awful eye, Mammy couldn't climb the step ladder, none of the grown-ups could, so I went there, and there I stayed all day.

Afterwards the others told me that Daddy was fearfully overcome when he saw her, and begged to be forgiven, he made her return to bed and sat beside her all day, at first she said she would leave him and return to Hillersdon, but he was so heartbroken she forgave him by about lunch time, I have rather an idea she enjoyed that first day with her black eye. Kathleen and Chloe did too, they told Miss Smith when she came that she was to go away and never come any more, the poor thing didn't know what to think, but in the end they convinced her and she left, it was a long time before a new governess came.

The black eye took ages to get better, we implored Mammy to keep to her room and not let any stray callers see it, at first she was good about this, and we told everyone she was away, unfortunatly a tennis party had been arranged that week and we had to go through with it, we were not experianced enough to know how to put it off. By this time she was getting jolly fed up with her bedroom and the big birds on the wall paper, so she threatened to appear, but eventually she promised to keep out of view and we felt we could breathe again.

Arriving guests seemed rather surprised as we explained her absence, people in villages just don't go away when they are going to give a tennis party, the whole thing has been arranged weeks ago and is all very formal, at least it was in those days. I guess some of them had heard about her eye because they kept wanting to know details of where she had gone and as each of us gave a different version of her visit, they asked more and more questions.

Mammy's bedroom overlooked the tennis court, she got pretty cross being shut up there missing all the fun (she thought it was fun) everyone looked as if they were enjoying themselves, she got more and more angry as she watched, then she suddenly appeared, she walked slowly down a nearby path, looking very like Hamlets father, then dissapeared again. The game of tennis came to an abrupt end, the onlookers turned their eyes to the place where Mammy had vanished, then they all started to talk together. A catty girl called Marjorie said

'There is your Mother, she must have returned unexpectedly, I must speak to her, how queer!' She hurried to the point where Mammy had vanished, fortunatly with no success, Mammy must have repented or lost her nerve, she didn't appear again, until they had all gone.

Dancing Class

Once a week, Mary, Beatrix and I were taken to dancing class in the assembly Rooms, we wore frilly white frocks made of silk, and bronze dancing pumps, we had to take swords with us, because a sword dance was one of the dances we were learning, we went on learning it for about two years, perhaps the mistress didn't know many dances. When there were enough children we did the lancers and Sir Rodger de Coverly, I found it much to difficult and always thought Sir Rodger de Coverly was a relation of St Vitus. Beatrix was the only one who was any good at dancing, she had a hero worship for the mistress, Miss Manin, so perhaps that helped her.

I hated dancing class so much and had a kind of sick feeling in the pit of my stomach before I went, I called it dancing class feeling, and still have it sometimes, when I'm applying for a job, or getting married and similar occasions.

The assembly rooms were over some shops and were drafty and unfinished looking, the room we danced in was often used as a rifle range, so sometimes there were lead pellets all over the floor Miss Manin would get someone from the shops to come with a broom and sweep them all away, this caused a welcome delay. The class was closed down before Kathleen and Chloe were old enough to attend, so they had to go to Swan Village by train once a week in Winter for their lesson. Quite often Mary would make me take them, the Swan Village class was much larger than the one in the Assembly rooms, Kathleen and Chloe would nearly die with shyness, Chloe was so stiff and tall, she looked like a totem pole, and poor Kathleen was scared stiff, and her brow was all puckered, she danced even worse than Chloe, once during a skipping dance, she caught a Mamas' fussy hat with her rope and it came flying off and got all squashed and trampled on. Another time they wore frightful hand knitted art silk frocks, very shiney and strangly heavy, as they danced or rather hopped about, their frocks stretched and stretched till they reached the ground, every one laughed except us, they didn't go any more after that.

Perfectly Beastly Frock

I didn't grow very quickly, and being in the middle of the family achieved a number of outgrown garments which caused me untold misery, I thought everyone in the village recognised them and were dispising me, sometimes Mammy went to the trouble of disguising them by dye, I remember being quite pleased with my new navy coat until Mary said with a sniff, 'Yah! its only my old one painted'

When we were small Mammy bought us rather nice clothes, handmade smocks, holland for the morning and silk in the afternoon, and we had really lovely scarlet capes with pointed hoods she had specially made from her design, but as we grew older she lost interest in our clothes, and our things just came in batches from a school outfitter, flannel shirts, gym frocks, kilted skirts, the usual dreary outfits English school girls have been wearing for the last thirty years. After we left school we were luckey if we had anything new at all, when we got too appaulingly shabby we ordered something ourselves, usually completely unsuitable and often in very bad taste, Mary managed to have a few quite nice things and her taste was better than ours, but she never gave us any advice, unless to encourage us to buy something really awfull. I always remember with shame how we all went to an otter hunt, Mary watched Beatrix and I start off dressed in artificial silk stockings which changed to cotton at the knee, brown velvet frocks trimmed with fur and straw hats, she said she would catch us up, but she didn't, when we arrived at the meet, there she was dressed all in brown tweed, with a felt hat and heavy brouges, all the other followers were dressed practically the same, we went up to her but she said 'I don't want you kids tagging along with me' Beatrix and I were overcome with shame but we were determined we were not going to return home, so we followed a few yards behind her, she kept throwing us furious glances, but we were glad to see no one took any more notice of her than of us, she sulked with us for days after.

One Autumn, just before we returned to school, Mammy fished out the most frightful navy dress of Beatrix's for me to wear, it was trimmed with black braid and had waddy slit arrangements for your bust (like old fashioned combs) I looked at it in horror, then flatly refused to wear it. Mammy lost her temper with me, but still I refused to put the beastly thing on, then she started screaming, so I screamed back, we were making such a noise Daddy came running to see what on earth was the matter, and before I quite realized what was happening he had put the fowl thing on me, I bit his hand, then ran away as fast as I could, I felt horrorably humilated and angry, I crossed my arms over the embarrising bust, and made for the engin-room. I sat there for a long time, no one came, I cried a lot and wished I was dead. I heard the gong go for lunch and

95

felt sadder still and hoped it wasn't chicken, after what seemed a very long time, I heard a scuffel up the steps, then Chloe pushed the door open 'I knew you would be here' she said 'I've saved some bread for you, its gone a bit dry because I had to hide it in my knickers, but dont expect you will notice if you are starving' I choked it down to show how starving I was, though I did think she wasnt very enterprising over her choice of food, jelly would have been nice, but would have made rather a mess of her knickers I supposed. Then she said 'If you are thinking of running away I'll come too, I'm so sick of Mary bossing around' (she had recently left school and having nothing to do all day was in her words trying to 'reform Kathleen and Chloe')

The running away idea appealed to me immensly, so we hurredly made plans, Chloe was to go back to the house and collect anything we owned of value that we could sell, we had no money atall, then she had got to bring sissers to cut off her hair, I don't know why her hair had got to be cut off, perhaps people in the books we read did that when they ran away from home, luckely she could not find any sissers so her beautiful plates were saved, she returned with a small pink and white basket of treasures, a heart shaped locket, a gold chain, a gold mounted tigers slaw, and an extinct sharks fossilised tooth, given me by an old professor and highly prized. It had started to drizzel, but we started off in high spirits, we were making for a small market town nine miles away, we believed we would get a job there on the stage, they had a pantomine there every Christmas for a week, we practiced the few dancing steps we knew as we walked the muddy road, it seemed a long, winding road, after about five miles we didn't dance any more, then we started to worry, perhaps we wouldn't get a job after all, maybe the shops would all be closed and we wouldnt be able to sell our jewels and would have no money to stay in a hotel, we realised with horror the awful fact that we had no nightdresses with us, that seemed the last straw, but still we walked on, rather slowly now. We began to get frit about what they would do when they discovered we had gone, every time we heard an approaching horse or car we hid in the hedge, we were sure they must be coming to look for us by now, what would they do to us if they caught us,? send us to prison most probably, perhaps for murder, the shock of us disapearing would be sure to kill Granny with her weak heart, and her death would be laid at our door, maybe she was dead now, Daddys' heart was weak too even if he didnt die he would doubtless have a stroke, and be all stiff for the rest of his life, Chloe and I would have to push him about in a long wheel chair for our punishment, we could see him, stiff and long, covered by a blanket, all you could see above was an enormouse black moustaches and a pair of fierce brown eyes that wouldn't move at all.

We got more and more depressed as we trudged on, it was raining heavily now, we came to a small village, suddenly we smelt an overwhealmly apertising smell, it came from a low brick hut, I peered through the steamy window, then called Chloe to come and look, there were trays and trays of bread and a man was just taking another large batch out of the oven, we felt we could eat the whole lot, we hadn't realised how hungry our long walk had made us, that was the kind of bread starving people think of, not a few dried up scraps that have been in someones knickers, we thought of the tea at home, they must be having it now, that is if they arn't all dead or anything, plates and plates of bread and butter, honey in the combe, at least three different cakes to choose from.

Perhaps we wouldnt get work in a pantomine after all, when our treasures were all sold we would starve, that is if we did not laungish in prison, if we went home now, straight away, we may be in time to save Grannys' life, at least we would be in time for supper. We started to run in the opersite direction to the one we had been going, we hurried and hurried but still we had miles to go, then a familar figure came sailing into sight on a bicycle, it was the old Doctors' wife, she did not seem particularly surprised to see us, beyond remarking on our mud spattered appearance, if there had been any deaths in our family surely the Doctors' wife would know, we felt heartened after that encounter, and it didn't take so very much longer to reach home after that, when we got there we sat on the front doorsteps for a time, but it was cold on our bottoms so we crept in and the first person we met was Mammy with her mouth all boxed up, she said 'your father wants to see you, he is in the billard-room' We went to the billard-room, there was daddy just removing the cloth off the table, he was evently having a few friends in that evening for a game and looked bored at the thought of rowing us, he just said 'you Little Varmets had better go to bed you have caused enough trouble for to-day' Chloe went to bed and cried herself to sleep, we didn't have any supper, on my way upstairs I noticed the gramophone was in the hall, I went downstairs again and put it on, I never dared to put it on usually in case it broke, but I wanted everyone in the house to know I wasnt going to be sent to bed like a baby and I didnt care a damn how angry the grown-ups were with me, I played record after record, much to tierd to notice what they were, when I just couldnt keep awake any more I went to bed, not before I just had a look round Grannys' door to make sure she was alright, as I was undressing the awful fact dawned on me I was still wearing that abominable frock.

Shooting

Daddy had a number of guns, he kept them in the billard-room, there was a revolver too, he was always threatning to shoot himself, his creditors or both with it, the big guns, some of them had double barrels to make it easy for bad shots and cross eyed men, they were intended for shooting game, although quite often they were used on cats and people, towards the end of his life he got obsessed with the idea of shooting my red setter. With horror I would see the barrel of a gun appearing from a holly bush, I would call her away with shaking voice, he would fire after us as we ran away, but fortunatly his aim had got rather bad by this time. Occaisionally he unsuccessfully tried shooting Mammy and as she was quite deaf she didn't even notice. Once he had a few shots at a cousin and the man she was engaged to because they stayed rather late on the river, they were frightfully upset and left the house early the next morning and we never saw them again, it was of no conciquence, because we didn't like them anyway, but Mary who was in the boat as well said it was rather an alarming experience, her heart sank when she saw Daddy prancing on the river bank in his nightshirt waving a gun above his head, as soon as he saw them in the moonlight he started firing like mad, perhaps he was mad, it took Palmer days to fill the holes in the side of the boat.

Before all this he was a good shot, and our larder was kept well stocked with game at the approate seasons, he shared rather a rough shoot with the two doctors and the vicar, Palmer who never got left out of anything went as loader, it was also his job to make and light a bonfire, they would cook ham on sticks over it and bake potoaes in the ash. When Mammy got shoot minded we would drive over in a pony and trap with Miss Glide and a huge hamper of lunch, it was rather fun till I heard a hare scream when it was shot.

Good Luck Numbers

When I was eight, I developed a kind of complex, I called it 'good luck numbers' and it made me touch and do every thing twice, I just hated doing it but felt awful bad luck would come if I didn't, it wasn't quite so bad touching things, but it got such a hold over me that if I accidently upset my milk, as soon as the table was mopped up and I was given some more, over it went again, for luck I thought, but no luck did it bring me, only great trouble from Miss Glide. Eventually it got so bad I had to breathe in twos and felt half sufercated, then one day as we were picking wallnuts I fell over the basket and upset them all, we all helped put them back in the basket and as soon as it was full over I kicked it, Miss Glide gave me a good shaking and smacked me too, after this if ever she caught me doing things twice I got smacked again, but for several years I still practiced good luck numbers secrectly, unfortunatly I gave the habit to Kathleen and Chloe, it didn't get such a grip with them and the grown-ups didn't notice.

One day I was hiding behind Mammy's chair in the morning-room and I heard her say to the-old-doctors-wife, that she got in such a bad state before Kathleen was born, each time she walked round the garden, she felt she must walk round the other way to undo herself. It was a great relief to know even grown-up people got these kind of feelings and somehow it helped me shake off good luck numbers and would scorn Kathleen and Chloe when I found them still under its spell.

There were other things that worried and frightened me too, prayers was one of them, if I ommitted to say them before I got into bed I felt God would do something frightful to me, so I would kneel in bed and say them, then on thinking it over just when I was warm and drousy in bed, I would worry in case God wouldn't approve of saying prayers in bed, so I would get out onto the cold lino and say them all over again, and they were such long prayers, I daren't leave anything out. Each year they grew longer, the 'our Father' part wasn't so bad, it was all the Dont Let parts that were so wearysome. Please God don't let the end of the World come, please God don't let the dogs get distemper, dont let me get cancer, dont let me get consumption or worms, please God don't let me grow up ugly or get a mastache or be an old maid, please God don't let me get vitrol, and so on. Vitrol was one of the horrors of my life, one morning Mary and Beatrix had taken me into the coach house and Mary said 'shall we tell the kid about vitrol,' I said I would give them four yellow snails if they would, so Mary told me there was some dreadful stuff called vitrol, if it fell on you it burnt you to pieces, the awful thing was it didn't always burn you straight away, sometimes years later you would find your self rotting away suddenly, you might touch something that had had vitrol on with out knowing at the time. I asked her where this awful stuff was, and she said Daddy had heaps of it, he used it to make the bells ring and quite a lot of it had been spilt about the house. A few days later she showed me one of the bound volumes of *Punch*, it had a great hole eaten into it, that is where Daddy dropped Vitrol she said and put it away. I was filled with horror, a horror which grew much worse at night, sometimes I would touch the afflicted *Punch* and run away screaming.

Potting Shed and Hen Pens

No actual potting took place in the potting shed it was really Palmers holy of holies and he liked to keep it locked as much as possible, if he was in an exceptionaly good mood he would let one of us in and give us an apple off the little tree outside, he cut the apples into small pieces with his penknife, they had a special taste of steel which made them different and more exciting than garden apples. Sometimes he would show us the stump of his thumb and tell us how it had got blown off by a gun backfiring when he was quite a boy, and how he had left school when he was only nine and got a job as gardener's boy and he had been the gardener of our garden for years and years, before Daddy had even bought the house. Because of this the garden seemed to belong more to him than to us, even Daddy was frit of him and let him have his own way in everything. He kept the greenhouses locked which annoyed Mammie terrably, once she managed to get the key and she went in and smashed every pot of flowers she could reach, he was so upset he cried and we all felt horrofied. One of the reasons Mammie felt so bitter about Palmer was because he wouldn't let her have a piece of the garden for herself 'he said he wouldn't have any bloody women mucking about his garden' Daddy let him have his way as usual but bought her some expensive books on gardening and she had to be content to read about gardening Another grudge Mammie had against Palmer was he had her little dog Dodo distroyed while she was in bed hatching Kathleen, he wasn't at all kind to animals and hated dogs worst of all.

The loss of a thumb didn't prevent Palmer from enjoying shooting, Daddy often took him with him as loader when he had a days shooting, but it usually resulted in Palmer shooting as much as anyone. Other times he would shoot sparrows from the potting shed door, we thought he used to cook them on the stove with a tortoise on and the words 'a slow but sure combustion' engraved on the top, when we went to boarding school there were the same stoves in the classrooms, no wonder, we said, we have such chillblains, just potting shed stoves are all we have to warm us. We hated it when we caught Palmer shooting the pidgeons, he said they had to be kept down, but it was always the young plump ones who were missing and the old ones died in the cote, when they were spring-cleaning the young birds would throw the old skeletons out down into the yard.

We were not supposed to play in the chicken pens, partly because Palmer didn't like it also they were very dirty and rather stiff with fleas, although I've found hen fleas don't bite much, and the ones off hedgehogs are alright too, rabbit and dog fleas bite like anything. There were four hen pens, two small ones for pullets and turkeys, and large ones that sloped down to the river for the old birds, I don't know why they had the best of everything. There was an old stone wall that devided them, once when I was very young about six I noticed a small green door with a rounded top in this wall, as I came nearer I saw it was open and the Big Bacon Cock was standing there welcombing hens from the other side, he shook hands or rather claws with each hen as she entered, then he looked at me in such a haughty manner that I felt ashamed and went away, I never saw the door again but Daddy and Palmer were annoyed at all the hens getting mixed like that.

Every morning after breakfast Granny would crunch small pieces of eggshell or something like that in her mouth, it sounded rather a comfortable thing to do like a cow chewing its cud, I tried it too but bits of shell got all stuck in my throat, so perhaps it was her false teeth, they didn't stay in very well although she used to stick them in with glue, sometimes they would fall out at dinner parties and she would have to dash into the pantry and stick them back, I hope I never have to wear them, false teeth, it must be grim. After Granny had sat chewing her cud a bit she would collect little pieces of toast and scraps left over from breakfast and mix them up in the silver bacon dish and take them down to the hens in the first pen, I used to go with her, the Bacon Cock would always get there first and she would empty the dish over him and the hens would peck it off, all the same he always got the most and grew enormouse, he was all shiney from the bacon fat and had beautiful long, blacky green feathers in his tail. There were al kinds of hens but not many of them still layed eggs, there were some who were fifteen years old, they were pale blue and a man who had afterwards died of cancer had given them to Mammy, so we always kept them in his memory.

The ducks lived on the edge of the tennis court behind wire netting untill they were too old to be eaten, then they were allowed on the river and had their meals with the hens, when she was older Kathleen used to look after the ducks, she always seemed to have a tame runt that lived in the house.

We had three peacocks, but two of them got drowned, the remaining one was called Phillip. he was very tame and handsome, Mammie once put a gold locket and chain round his neck because she had read about a peacock like that, but he didn't like it and pecked it off, he used to sleep in a tree which overhung the river and in the daytime an owl lived there. He spent much of his time in the hen pens and eventually one of the hens layed an egg as large as a pecocks, so we asked a friend to hatch it in his incubator to see what would come out, it was a pity that it burst and spoilt a lot of his eggs.

We used to have Phillip in the house quite a lot, one day at lunch time he turned round in a hurry and set his tale alight from the diningroom fire, we didn't have him in much after that except in the billardroom where there was central heating, he would walk around pecking the carpet while Daddy wrote letters there.

Aunts Arriving

Sometimes an awful lot of cleaning and cooking went on in the house, and Mammy would brush our hair with a silver brush with angles head on, she brushed very hard and made a hissing noise between her teeth, all our clothes were clean right down to our skin although it wasn't Sunday, all this usually meant an invaison of Aunts and cousins was expected from Hillersdon. The arrival took place before lunch, and as soon as they were in the hall Mammy hurried to welcome them, Granny tripping behind, very hostile with her jaw sticking out, we stayed in the morning-room, it was a good chance to eat the ginger biscuits, but they soon trooped in. 'Well, Well, we are here at last, how are you Margie dear, you look a little peaked I must say, over doing it, I expect, no wonder with all those great girls, you should get Mary to help you' etc. There was a lot of conversation in this strain, and uplifting of vails and loosening of furs and scarves went on, at this moment Daddy used to appear with a tray of drinks, their desire for a warming drink made their greeting of him more cordial than usual. The Aunts drank whiskey and said they felt a little better, but it had been a terrable journey and they must leave before tea because the chauffer didn't like driving in the dark (they lived twenty miles away) Then they started to notice us and very occasionally one of the cousins was sent back to the car to fetch toys or sweets that had been brought for us. The girl cousins were mostly older than we were, rather anemic and very self conscious and nervy, I think their mother made them get like that, they were inclined to be spiteful too. one used to bring a camera and take waddy snapshots of us in groups. The boy cousins didn't come often, and when they did they were frankly bored with us, one called Cyril in particular, we called him Snivvel on every occaison, secretly I thought him rather handsome, but knew Mary would be scornful if I admitted it.

Mary wasn't poplar with the Aunts, she was rather haughty with them and answered catty remarks in kind. They quite liked me because I was friendly and rather pretty, but a lot of 'you look just like your father' went on, I knew that was a bad thing to have said about one. Sometimes they took me back to Hillersdon with them in the car, I used to feel awfully excited on the journey there, but on arrival felt dreadfully homesick and lonely. The days there seemed so dreary, I never remember the sun shining, the garden paths were all made of gray brick and the box hedging was so high you couldn't see the flowers, the stables were the only homely place there and the grooms were nice too. All the family used to go out most of the day riding and in season hunting or shooting, at least all the family except the camera one, she was too nervouse to ride and spent most of her time talking to the maids and repeating everything they said to Auntie Teania or poking her nose into the cottages, looking at their babies and explaining who I was 'You remember my poor cousin Margey, well, this one of her little girls, you wouldn't think so, would you' and they would say they could remember Mammy when she was just the same age as me, then we would have to drink tea with condenced milk in it, very sweet condenced milk, which had the inevitable babies dummy dipped in it from time to time, after that we would go to another cottage and the same thing would happen all over again. She was batts – the camera cousin.

After I'd been at Hillersdon a week or so Mammy would come to fetch me away, she was always on her best behaviour there, and enjoyed calling on the people she used to know as a girl, she liked talking to the old grooms too, they could remember her when she was a little girl and this pleased her very much. She always took all her best clothes on these visits, the cousins admired them, their clothes were very wholsome, she would give them some of the things they seemed to want so much and when she went home without them Mary was cross, she had so few nice things herself.

Although Mammy loved being at her old home so much, she wouldn't stay there long, they were all very kind to her, but for some reason she always hurried back home, when she got there she was unbearable for the first few days, Daddy, the house and all of us children were beneath contempt, but after about a week she settled down.

When we were older our visits to Hillersdon changed, for one thing we had to sleep at Aunt Evas' house and have most of our meals there, I hated this so much, when I did go to the big house for any meals if visitors were there I would just be introduced as 'Oh, this is my little niece' even when I was about eighteen, at dinner I was never asked what I would like, if it was chicken Uncle Jack would put just sausages on my plate, or if there were lovely homemade marangues and a floppy looking jelly, all I got was the jelly, no wine ever came my way either. If I started to talk Aunt Teana would surely think of some humilating thing to say and the batty cousin would enter into this sport, she loved to think of someone else being bullied for a change.

After we were older the cousin we used to call Snivvel used to say come and see the cellers with me, but I only went once, so he was more bored than ever with me.

Food

We used to go on strike if meals were served we didn't approve of, we didn't call it going on strike, we would hear Daddy and Granny talking about strikes, but I always thought it was a lot of fierce men with black mastarches all striking giant matches on an enormous door, and in the background someone chanting 'Hark, hark the dogs do bark, the beggers are come to town' Our strike was always caused by animals we were fond of being killed to be eaten. We didn't mind the ducks and chickens been killed in the ordinary way, but the ones who had been weakly and reared in the kitchen were quite different, every year there were several rickety ducklings who became pets, but they were all eaten in the end, I suppose Daddy couldn't keep lots of ducks eating their bills off all the winter, but we thought at least they could have sold them or something. Once when Aunt Fred of the seal-like feet was staying she kept complaining about the noise the guinea fowl made, there were three of them, one a beautiful grey called Mrs Fosebroke, they were all killed, and she helped the grown-ups eat them, we had always hated her, but now we hated her worse. We didn't come into lunch that day, but expect we eat some of the poor birds afterwards in mince or something. One day when I was in the larder helping myself to milk, I looked in the big wooden safe where the bread usually lived, but instead of bread, there was a fat little dead pig, it looked so clean and sweet, but of course the grown-ups eat him, we all stayed out in the stables that day and eat dog biscuits, I guess we were eating horse really, they didn't mind us not coming in, they were glad I expect to be able to sit munching piglet all on their own.

Sometimes if Mammy had been reading a book about actors, she would say she was a true Bohemian and loved tripe and onions, so she and Daddy would have it for supper, if the actors she had been reading about had been quite rich, they would eat stout and oysters instead, they used to come in a little barrel by train, and Palmer would have to fetch them.

On the whole we had very good food, Mammy loved cooking and had many books of reciepts she had been collecting ever since she was a child, she was very extragavant and made masses of work, but the results were good, we had a cook but if there was anything exciting to be cooked Mammy always did it, it must have been maddening for the cook. Granny could only make two things, toffee and currant biscuits, both were lovely, but how she made them was kept a secret, she used to make patent medicenes, well not patent, home made ones, but that wasn't exactly cooking. When Mammy made cakes she would let me help, sometimes I would be allowed to make quaker oat cakes entirely by myself. Now I can cook anything, plum puddings, jam, pork pies, bread, turkey, and it all started with Quaker Oat cakes – the Vicarage reciept.

Bother-em-Dick

Bother-em-Dick lived with the Old Soldier in a small house on the Gorse Road, he was only four feet high and had a long beard, which grew down as far as his knees, on his head grew a green pork-pie hat, his clothes were a kind of purple and they looked as if they grew out of him too, perhaps they did because he always wore the same ones. When he walked his feet made no noise at all, he must have been rather shy about this because he always whistled a little tune to let you know he was coming in a very soft, low little whistle. The village people were terrified of him, and so were we, they said he did awful things in the churchyard at night, he was called the local war-lock, but he was really a locksmith, no one dared to go to him to have their keys made except Granny, Daddy once locked the Billard-room and took the key to Birmingham, when Granny found out she got Bother-em-Dick to come and make a new one, she wanted to watch him work, but he wouldn't allow her to, he just slipped away without being paid, leaving a beautiful green key in the door. When Daddy returned home he was as angry as a bear and broke the key to pieces and threw the bits out of the window, and where they fell a small tree shaped like an umbrella grew, the dogs were always fed under that tree with the bones and things left over from our dinner.

People wern't frit of the Old Soldier, they would buy him tobacco and things, no one liked to ask him what it was like living with Bother-em-Dick

Maids in the Kitchen

I liked to sit on the kitchen fender and listen to the maids talking 'Miss Mary is on her high horse again' they would say, and I could imagine her on a giant clothes horse cantering about the house. Once they said 'anyone can tell the Master has a touch of the Tarbrish (tarbrush) and its come out in Miss Kathleen and Barbara' I thought how strange to be Tarbrish and know nothing about it before, I told Beatrix about it and we talked about it a lot. My first term at school I told everyone I was Tarbrish really but it was a secret, fortunatly no one knew what I was talking about, they just thought it was the mad kind of thing a new girl would say.

Mammy was very easy going with the maids, they had masses of time off, and could stay out as late as they liked, so they often had babies, we never knew they were having them till they were almost due and the-old-doctors-wife would come and tell Mammy and the poor girl would have to go, their Mothers would come and cry and say they had no idea their Annie was in the family way, but they usually got married in the end, it was luckey no one thought they were Daddies babies. We had a poor little cook called Lilly, she was as ugly as a witch but had beautiful long golden hair right down to her poor little black boots, she was only four feet three. She had had a sad life and been abandoned by her parents when she was a young child and been brought up by relations who did not want her, she already had a little boy when she came to us, but she was a very good cook so Mammy didn't say anything about it, but after a time she started another, she used to sit all huddled up by the kitchen fire holding the monkeys hand and looking so unhappy, but we didn't realize what was the matter till one of the local good wives told Mammy, her sister refused to have her home and no where could be found for her, so eventually she had to go to the workhouse where she had twins.

The maids always hated Granny because she was so horrible to them, they used to put cold hotwater bottles in her bed and drink her whiskey, and snatch the vegetables away before she had helped herself. Often in the middle of meals Granny's teeth would fall out and she would dash from the diningroom to the pantry and stick them in with some glue stuff she kept in there, if the maids were washing up they would shreak with laughter, and Granny would call them insolent chits, and come back with her jaw all trembling.

Our kitchen had a dusty hot cross bun hanging from the ceiling, every good Friday they put up a new one, the old one turned into a kind of mummy, there were hams hanging up too and a side of bacon, Palmer cured the pigs in the saddle room in a large zinc trough, the maids said you mustn't watch him if you had a period or the hams would get bewitched and go all wrong, Mammy said this too. There were three kitchens altogether, all leading out of each other, they had stone floors with wells in the middle, they used to have their meals in the hot cross bun kitchen because there was a huge Eagle range there which heated the water and did the cooking, once a rat fell down the chimney right into the porrage, I've never eaten any since because it always seems to smell ratty.

We liked having tea with the maids, they gave us biscuits floating in our cups of tea and they always eat heaps of vinager, after tea they used to sing, songs about dark eyed lovers, they always sounded like hymns.

Bees

We used to eat heaps of honey in combs and it was lovely. Palmer looked after the bees, they were nice friendly bees with kind faces, and they never stung us, their hive was by the tree lupins, and they made as much honey as we could possibly manage to eat and never seemed to swarm in the middle of tennis parties like most peoples bees do. But one day they all fell down dead and they had got a disease called Isle of White, so we didn't have any more bees. Then Palmer started saying the garden needed them, so the bee man came with some more in a sack, he also brought rather a pretty daughter with him, but she had a humped back, it suddenly started to come when she was ten years old and they couldnt get rid of it, still she had a nice face. When the beeman and his daughter arrived there was a great argument between Daddy, Mammy and Palmer, Mammy wanted the bees where they had always been – by the tree lupins, but Daddy and Palmer said the river path was the place, and the hive was moved there. The beeman tipped a great bundle of bees at the foot of the hive and a pastry board was placed for them to walk up, and they swarmed up without any hesitation. All the time Mammy kept saying the wasps had so many nests in the river bank they would surely kill the bees and the hive MUST be moved, and she just went on and on about it moping and mowing and wailing away, and Palmer was growling away to himself, and Daddy swearing not to himself, then he grew awfully fierce and picked up the hive and shook the poor bees all over her she screamed and cried and really tore her hair and ran towards the house casting her bee covered clothes as she went, but she didn't die or any thing frightful like that, she only had about ten stings which was a mercy. Daddy was left holding the bee hive, then they started to sting him too, so he put it down and the remaining bees walked in as if nothing had happened, but the thought of bees made us rather sad now, and within a few days the wasps had turned them all out.

Wicked Foxes and Engines

The moment a fox came into a dream it turned into a nightmare, dreadful things started to happen, horrorfing things, decomposing bodies that smelt all sweet and frightful and you woke up feeling it must be true, everything was disgusting and the world would never get right again, you shook so much your teeth chattered. Dreams about engines turned to nightmares too, they made frightful noises in your head and were enormous and caught you and you were dragged down among crushing wheels and giant belts, you couldn't breath at all and suddenly you would be awake to find the bedclothes all over your face and your heart would be beating very quick, but it wasn't an evel dream like foxes.

When I was about eight a wicked little fox started to appear in my dream, instead of letting him make frightful things happen I walked boldly up to him and said 'Knickerbockers' and he just slunk away and no more foxes ever came to me at night. I told Beatrix about this and she said she could stop nightmares by shaking herself and saying I know you are not true, you are only a silly old dream and then she would wake up. I tried this and it was most successful and gradually I almost ceased to have nightmares. Some dreams were lovely, I still have one that I'm swimming in deep, still water among fantastic fish, the more I look at them the larger and more queer they look and I love them dearly almost more intencely than I love things when I am awake, Kathleen has a dream almost similar to this, perhaps because we used to spend so much time fishing.

To dream of food is always disipointing, it looks so apertising but when you come to eat it, it just doesn't taste of anything. Sometimes if I had a particularly good dream I would try to will myself to go on where I left off the next night, but it didn't often work or if it did it was just a pale reflection of the original.

Chloe used to walk in her sleep, one night she walked into Kathleens bedroom, Kathleen thought she was a ghost and pushed her out, she fell down the stairs, after that she had to stay in bed for about a year and it was simply ages before she could walk again, but it wasn't Kathleens fault really it turned out she had got rehumatic fever from playing in the woodshed.

Gather your hats while you may

One day as we were playing Beatrix and I found a large branch with a lot of twigs trailing from it, we both got astride it and pretended it was a horse, then we found ourselves slowly raising from the ground, soon we were flying through the sky, we were not at all afraid, it seemed quite an ordinary thing to happen, there was our house quite tiny down below, with the silver river twisting beside it, up we went till we could only see clowds below, then we came to a little red house, it was very clean, a fairy lived there and she was pleaded to see us, her eyes were made of looking glass but she was a bit little. The house was rather like Palmers' with out the beastly little black and tan dog that barked, there were bright wool mats and lovely wax fruit in glass cases, a tinker bell in the window and varses like chandeers. We liked it there and often travelled on the magic stick always to the little red house, then Mary got cross about it and broke the magic stick, we tried sitting on the stokehole wall and shutting our eyes and willing ourselves to go up into the sky but we never could again. We were about five or six at the time.

Sometimes other magic kind of things happened at this period, one night for some reason Beatrix and I were put to sleep in one of the maids bedrooms, both in the same big bed, being in a strange room we couldn't sleep and lay side by side gazing out of the window at the summer sky, it was still quite light, suddenly to our surprise we saw an enormouse hat come floating past our window, we both cried out together 'Look at that hat! We had hardly recovered from the surprise, when more and more and more hats came tumbeling out of the sky, blue hats, hats with large spots, pink hats, they all came tumbeling down, they were rather a mushroomy shape, eventually we fell asleep watching them, but if only we had got out of bed and gone outside to see those hats all heaped up and perhaps taken a few back with us, we were too frit of Miss Vann to do this, needless to say the next morning the first thing we did was to get out of bed and look out of the window, of course there was not a hat to be seen, that just goes to prove you should gather your rosebuds while you may.

Mr Ellismore!
How is your window looking?

'What has Mr Ellismore got in his window Kathleen, are the village windows all decorated yet?' Chloe would ask during the years she was a cripple and had to rely on Kathleen for outside news. We were always more excited by the village shops than the large ones in Birmingham, I used to buy presants for the whole family, maids included, for about one shilling. A hankey with a carol printed on it for Mammy, pipe cleaners for Daddy, once Mrs Bennet-the-Barber forced me to buy some mastache wax, as I bought it I felt it was a dreadfully waddy thing to give anyone, but Daddy said it was just what he wanted. Mrs Bennet-the-Barber also had a very fine line in penny scent, it was in powder form and you mixed it yourself at home, Granny usually came in for the scent, it was bright green. The maids had halfpenny rings, and we sisters exchanged penny toys, except Mary who sometimes sewed us things, they were sewn with tiny stitches, but never completely finished, pinifores without buttons and button holes, peticoats with the tucks only tacked, we never really wore them, all the same it was nice to look at the small stitches, like a good example.

Mammy did her Christmas shopping in Birmingham, she paid about two visits just before Christmas, taking Miss Glide or who ever the reigning governess was, and as many children as she could manage. She loved Christmas, the shopping, cooking and general bustle made her excited and happy. The shops in Birmingham seemed huge and wonderful to us, but almost too good to be true, like another world. Mammy was such a good customer in the grocers stores that there was a special man who could talk on his fingers to her, he conducted her from department to department, filling the pages in his order book. We children followed, almost anything we admired was added to the list, dozens of boxes of fantastic crackers, there were elvas plums, christalized fruit in wooden boxes, stuffed dates, and my favourate maron glaces, Greek honey, halva, olives, boxes of tangerenes, peaches and almonds and dried fruit, York hams, and all the other lovely Christmas things, they were all put down in the order book. I think it was the best smelling shop I have ever been in, our supper biscuits came from there, they were teddy bears, about three inches high, it seemed almost cruel to eat them.

After smelling all those good things we were hungry and wanted our lunch. Sometimes we had it in a large hotel, stiff with red carpets, waiters and palms, Mammy enjoyed places like that, but if she had too many children with her, we went to a more homely place, and would be served by brown clad middle aged waitresses with buns on their heads, they remembered us all by name, and said how much we had grown. We would eat enormous quantaties of rolls which seemed a very unusual and exciting kind of bread to us.

We so loved the large arcades which Birmingham seems to specialise in, in one, outside a fur shop there was a real stuffed mother bear smacking a baby bear across her knee, the day did not seem complete unless we paid them a visit. Somehow, without our knowledge, Mammy managed to order us numerous toys, our Christmas presants were always a complete surprise, and until I was twelve, I believed without any doubt that Santa Clause filled our stockings. The Christmas stockings were made of red flannel, and were more like sacks than stockings, about a week before Christmas they were handed out, I took mine to bed every night until Christmas Eve, then it was hung up, first on the end of the bed, how awful if it wasn't seen there, in pictures stockings were often hung from the mantlepiece, I would get out of bed and try this, then the door knob, soon I would be out of bed again. How on earth could he see it when he opened the door, perhaps the end of the bed was best after all, and I would start all over again. Sometimes I would put a mince pie by the stocking, once Mary had left one, and in the morning a bite was missing. I used to lie in bed, almost too excited to breathe, hoping and hoping I really would see Santa Clause this time, but I never did, although I kept the light on all night, covering my face with the eiderdown, and using the ventilation holes to spy through. Although I was always sure I hadn't been to sleep, I would suddenly notice the shape of the stocking had become quite different, very bulky, and a pile of boxes and parcels underneath. I could hardly bear to open the stocking, but would lie in bed imagining what all those enchanting buldges could be. When it really came to opening, Beatrix and I usually shared the excitement together, and a heavenly smell of spice, tinsel, new books and fruit seemed to come. When our beds were strewn with the contents of our stockings, open jack-in-a-boxes, dolls and teasets all jumbled up together, and a miniture Christmas pudding, there was always one of those in the toe of our stockings, with the orange and new pennies and nuts, when all these things had been examined, there were still the parcels from various relations to be unwrapped. The most exciting looking parcel which I had saved until the last, often turned out to disipointing, writing paper, a sealing set, or something dull, and the queer little packet you nearly forgot to open, would turn out to be something really lovely, like a glass ball with a snow storm inside, or a tiny horse made of real skin with leather harness. Granny always gave us an annual. The grown-ups never made the awful mistake of putting relations presants in our stockings, this ruins ones faith in Santa Clause in one blow.

When the thrill of our new treasures wore off a little, we would wake up Kathleen and Chloe to see what they had, Mary just stayed in her own room, we didn't dare to disturb her. When it was growing light, we used to take all our toys to show to Daddy and Mammy, they seemed to be amaised at all the things that had come out of our stockings, Christmas was one of the few times Mammy wasn't all strained and shy of us.

Breakfast was laid in the morning-room on Christmas – always sausages, the surplus from the turkey I suppose. After breakfast we didn't go to church like most people seem to, we just played in the drawing-room, we each took a corner to keep our new toys in, later on, some of the people who had been to church called on their way home, they drank sherry and admired our presants Mammy spent most of the morning arranging the table, she liked to do this and made it look really beautiful with flowers and fruit, and small silver dishes filled with delicious things. Canteens of the best silver were dug up from oak chests, and the Crown Derby china taken down from high pantry shelves, and the best linen came down from the chest on the landing, all to be returned the next day, until another great occasion waranteed their resection.

We had our Christmas dinner in the middle of the day, and an enormous amount was eaten and drunk, even we children were allowed wine. When it came to the pudding part, I was scared in case I got the thimble, and had to be a governess when I grew up, once I got the bachlors button, but everyone knows this isn't so bad.

The rest of the day unless there were visitors fell rather flat, we didn't have a tree, except sometimes for poor children in the village. There were quite a lot of carol singers, and we used to give them pennies and mince pies, that were left in the hall for them, but their singing always rather depressed me. The Grown-ups wakened up a little towards the evening, and came downstairs all in evening dress, so we had to get into the frocks we wore for dancing class. I took a kind of pride in seeing how late I would be allowed to stay on Christmas night, but I was always very tierd, and glad underneath when they sent me to bed, as long as Beatrix didn't stay up later than me, it was such a long day, and there was always tomorrow.

New Year

The new year wasn't nice at our house, the grown-ups got simply frightful, they all drank too much and got depressed, I can't think why they did, if it made them unhappy, Daddy was the worst, he would get all sentimental and morbid and keep saying this was the last year we would spend in the house, and we could expect the bailiffs any day now and Granny and Mammy would cry and have another drink to help them to bear up, then Granny and Daddy would both say 'This is the last New Year we shall see, they could feel Death coming nearer' and Granny would cry more than ever and say no one wanted you when you were old, and they never told you anything, and young people were hard and looked like strumpets anyway.

By this time there was an awful feeling of doom about, and I always felt particularly doomed because I hadn't eaten twelve mince pies between Christmas day and the New year, so I had no hope of twelve happy months, I was the only one who couldn't manage mincepies, they tasted horred and it wasn't much good eating them because they always came up again.

Just before twelve there was an interuption in our misery (perhaps Daddy's trouble was incometax, I've never paid any but I know people who do hate it) The intruption was Will Gardiner come to let the New Year in, he had red hair and if you dont have a red haired person to let the New Year in you are in for the most awful time, once we didn't and of course dreadful things did happen Daddy fell down dead and we had to leave the house and have no money, just the kind of things Daddy had been dreading. Will Gardiner had a Gang and before he did his magic they had to sing carols in harmony, it always made my tummy feel queer, and it was a relief when Will Gardiner came in and blessed the house, things began to brighten up, and they drank beer and eat mincepies and the grown-ups forgot how miserable they were and we remembered there were still two more weeks of the holidays left, and things became quite normal again.

Two Friends

We were not clever at making friends, partly because Mary was so scornful of most people, so we dardn't say we liked anyone very much in case we were included in her scorn, Daddy was rather a problem too, also both Daddy and Mammie were jealous and resentful if we got intimate with any other family. When we went to visit anyone we usually just pretended we were taking the dogs for a walk or if they found out where we had been we would deride our friends houses and gardens and say they were simply frightful compared to our own home, and anyway they were perfectly beastly people, all the same I made two great friends. The first friendship was when I was fairly young about ten I should think, we had been without a governess for rather a long time and Daddy and several other local parents got together and thought it would be a good idea to start a small private school consisting of about ten children. So after a lot of talk two rooms in a villa on the Gorse Road were taken for the school and a teacher called Miss Jones was engaged, Miss Jones was Welsh, she wore those awful rimless glasses, pence neze or something they are called, she resembled a goat in nearly every respect, she was really so goatish it hardly seemed possible, I dont think she had hoofs for feet, but of course they may have been disguised by her shoes, the pupels of her eyes went longways, and when she chewed her 'elevens' her jaw went a different way to her face, just the same way as a goats does, she always wore very bright green plaid clothes.

Mary and Beatrix were already at boarding school so we three younger ones had to attend this odd little school, there were also the vicars two small boys, a strange dark boy who never wore socks or an overcoat even in the snow, a fat little girl called Mary Buss, she had long thin pigtails and was very good at her lessons, and Lotty of the golden curls and cherubin red cheeks.

I was the eldest pupel and found the lessons very easy and dull, the other children seemed to be bored too and often went to sleep, so did Miss Jones, but when we wern't asleep there were several diversians, one was Miss Jones switch, not a thing to smack us with, but an awful piece of false hair which she wore draped across her head, it had kind of waxed and strung ends which came out on either side of her cheek, the great thing was to make it fall off, either by making her play violent games at playtime or with a pencil or ruler at lesson time, as a matter of fact it never did come right off but was often considerably disaranged and just hanging by a few hairs, she had false teeth but we left them alone, they wern't such a novilty as the switch. The other diversion was trying to spot the poor crazy girl in the next garden through the hedge, there were rather a lot of mad girls in the village but Jenny was the most interesting because she had glamour, apparantly she had been a beautiful, good little girl, but one day she went for a walk all by herself and a wicked man jumped out of a hedge and she was instantly changed into a fat ugly creature with a wisp of hair sticking out behind, an awful twisted mouth and large white eyes, the pupels all turned up, we were kind of frightened yet fasinated by her, poor creature.

It was of course little Lotty with her golden hair and Mamas' darling ways that became my first friend, I thought she was the most beautiful thing I'd ever seen, she lived only about three miles away, but somehow I had never set eyes on her until that first day I went to school, and then my eyes quite ached from looking at her so much. We were about the same age and soon became friendly, after a few weeks I asked her home to tea, I introduced her to the family with great pride, I particularly wanted to impress Mary and Beatrix who were home from school, by her great beauty, but on the contary, they all dispised her wholeheartedly, they always did dispise anyone with fair hair anyway, I should have remembered this, but it wasn't only the hair, every thing about her they hated, the grown-ups said she was smug and would look hideous when she grew up, her ankles were thick and anyone could see her nose would develop into a snout, Mary and Beatrix said she was a placid little bore, there were heaps of girls like that at school but no one took any notice of them, it was all most disipointing. still I brought her home fairly frequently, I often went to her home, I quite enjoyed it in a way but was afraid of her mother, who had rather a sly face and made catty remarks, she adored Lotty. I was glad to see her house was smaller than ours, I felt my appearance was so inferiour, black hair, brown eyes and pale brown face, and there were four more faces almost the same at home, so it evened things up a bit, having a more imposing home, perhaps not so quiert and respectable as Lotty's. Her parents were very well behaved, her father in particular, he was meek and good, sometimes he would bath his little daughter, this rather disgusted me somehow, then I began to notice she looked as if she drank too much milk, kind of stiff with it, around her rosy lips there was often a rim of milk and I began to imagine she smelt of it. I found I was getting very tierd of her, in fact I hated the poor girl, I felt all sufercated when I thought of her, and wondered how on earth I could stop knowing her. Strangely enough, Mammie who had disliked my friendship at first, now was always saying, 'do have dear little Lotty to tea, surely I havn't a fickle little girl,' hardly a day passed without Mammie pestering me about her. Luckely my fickelness coincided with the close of Miss Jones school, after that it was fairly easy to sever the friendship, although Mammie taunted me with Lotty for several years.

I don't know what caused the school to close down, it only lasted about two terms, perhaps Miss Jones was found unsuitable, when she first came she was often asked to tea or lunch, then they didn't ask her at all, the first time she came Kathleen did something that shocked the grown-ups rather a lot, as soon as Nora showed her into the drawing-room, Kathleen took one look at her, then turned her back, bent down, and pulling down her knickers, said 'Here, take that to your welcome' There was an awful fuss about it but we children were delighted, and treated her as a heroine, I even gave her one of my best books, about a girl who got her head stuck in a honey pot, and when they pulled her out her head had grown the same shape as the pot, then she listened at the door and her ear grew enormouse, it didnt mention about girls who showed their bottoms.

I made my second friendship when I was much older, I'd just left school and time was hanging rather heavily on my hands, I took the dogs long walks, read books, arranged fresh flowers in my bedroom every day, read and tried to write poetry, but still the days were very long. Mrs Clare came as a kind of Godsend to me, she must have taken pity on me or something, I can't think what she could find in the companionship of a dull and ignorant girl, fourteen years her juniour. She was about thirty, pretty in a large classical way, happily married, with two children, her husband was like a very dry piece of toast, a quiet, self contained man, but his wife loved to talk, how she talked! more words to a minute than any woman on earth, I just listened and listened, so perhaps that explained our strange friendship, also we were both rather dog crazy. Mrs Clare had recently started a kennel of sealyhams and in a few months I'd followed suit, none of our dogs ever won a prize and the puppies were sold for almost nothing, but they kept us busy and happy. Each morning I called at her house and off we went for a walk together, we talked and talked while the dogs got all tangled up on their leads or got lost or worst still killed chickens, Mary always found out about the chickens, although we paid for the damage, she always told Daddy all the awful things my dogs did.

I had tea at Mrs Clares' most afternoons, she lived in a bungalow on her husbands chicken farm, it was very ordinary but

I loved to go there so much, everything that belonged to her became wonderful to me even the children shared some of her reflected glory, and I liked to help her to put them to bed, she had a maid and a woman came in to do the cooking, so she too had time on her hands until she took up dogs and me. Quite often she came to tea at our house, and when we had dinner parties she and her husband were often asked, Mr Clare came in the evenings sometimes to play billards with Daddy, they knew about Daddy drinking and all those awful kind of things that happened in our house, and said I wasn't to worry about it. Daddy quite liked her, and made an effort to keep fairly sober when she was there, of course Mammie and Mary hated her, but nothing they could say or do made the least difference to my infatuation.

Things at home were getting pretty grim about this time, Daddy was particularly morose and glum through money worries, then he would drink and try and forget but it only made things worse, he never got jolly when he drank, just miserable, I can't think why he did it. Mammie was always quarreling with him, they were the two best people at agvergating each other I have ever met, she was getting awfully sick of us too, more even than usual, she had got an awful new habit of thinking people were falling in love with her, it was very trying and embarising, we would come on her gazeing into space, her lips moving in an imaginary conversation with a ficticious lover, she even went so far as to tell Daddy she had lovers and was unfaithful to him, this caused the most frightful rows, usually ending in him throwing all her clothes out of her bedroom window or Mammie running down to the river bank screaming and saying she was going to drown herself, sometimes waving an unloaded revolver above her head, but she never did commit suicide, sometimes the maids, if they were new, would run after her and drag her back to the house, but we would just sit on the chicken pen roof or somewhere peaceful. Added to these disturbances, there were the usual quarrels about money, when Mammie hadn't borrowed it, he carried his revolver in his pocket, we hoped it was unloaded, it was either to shoot the bailiffs with if they suddenly arrived in a body, as he was always expecting them to, or himself, he would never say which, perhaps he hadn't made up his mind. Anyway it was a releaf to get away from it all to the Clares quiet little house.

When I'd been friendly with them for just over a year I went for a visit to Hillersdon, it was pretty frightful there as usual, I only went because Mammie would have been so offended if I hadn't, and to get away from things a bit.

While I was there I went to a dog show, there I fell in love with a beautiful sealyham bitch, who was for sale at the very reasonable price of £15, she had won several minor prizes but was handicaped by rather light eyes, I felt I just must have her, at the back of my mind was the thought of Mrs Clares' surprise and envy when I arrived with this parigon of dogs. Mary lent me the money, she was always generous with any money she had, so I brought the bitch, who happened to have the frightful name of Firescreen Betty. I stayed longer at Hillersdon than I had intended, to have Betty mated to a dog at the kennels, I hoped I would make a fortune with her puppies and found a kennel of champions.

When I returned home I was rather horrorfied to see how Daddy had changed, he seemed years older, all shrunken and almost doddering, Mammie and Beatrix were in a frightful state of nerves, Beatrix had grown awfully nervy and highly strung lately, and she got on very badly with Mary, she spent hours practicing her violin, she didn't play very well and Mary teased her about that, sometimes she would lock herself in the billard-room and play highbrow music on the gramophone, Mary said it sounded as if a bloody battle was going on. Although it was nearly two years since Chloe had rhumatic fever she was still an invaled, she could only walk a few steps and suffered with her heart, she had grown very tall and thin, she was already the tallest of us all although she was the youngest, she looked very beautiful but rather as if she lived down a well, her long black plats hung down almost to her knees, and she was very lifeless, she was my favourite sister, and I felt very worried about her, altogether it was a dreary household I came back to, Kathleen and Mary were the only normal people, and they wern't very normal compared to ordinary people. I was glad to get out of the house the next morning and hurried off to Mrs Clare to exhibit the peerless Firescreen Betty, she had been expertly trimmed and looked as if she had been dressed by Worth or Norman Hartnell compared to our home trimmed dogs, who looked rather as if the mice had been gnawing their coats. I hadn't written to her about my purchase and hoped she would come to the door herself in answer to my ring, but it was the maid, she told me Mrs Clare was down in the yard with the car, I said 'Oh yes,' and started to walk towards the yard, then I suddenly thought Car!

they havnt got a car, what on earth is she talking about, then I reached the yard and there she was bending over a shining new car, a book of rules in one hand and a grease gun in the other. She seemed quite pleased to see me, and explained about the car, she had just bought it, wasn't it thrilling, she was having her first driving lesson that afternoon, she was simply mad about cars, then she noticed Betty, she said she was a sweet little dog, she quite showed ours up, didnt she? for her part she was giving the kennels up, just keeping old Flossy as a pet, they had been a great tie and expense, and already she had found homes for three of the puppies, and if nessesety she'd give the others away. Then I had to sit in the car and see how comfortable it was, I was shown the engine, and the beautiful box of tools, for the rest of the morning I heard all about how heavenly cars were, then Firescreen Betty and I went home.

Cut her hair long

Every Sunday a little barber with a deep dent in his head used to come to trim our hair, the dent was caused by a pewter pint mug in a fight, he was very bald and it frightened me to see his scull all crushed like that. He used to cut Daddies hair first and any of us who wanted a trim went to him, he operated in the conservotry, because it was easy to sweep up all the hair on the tiled floor. The grown-ups had read in the bible about a womans glory being her hair and they thought God would do something drastic if we had our hair cut short, they were always expecting God to do dreadful things, never to be a help. We had to wear our hair in pigtails, or if we had curly hair like Kathleen and I, it just hung in a lions main.

When I was fifteen, I had to go to the nearest town to do some shopping, I took Kathleen with me because Mammy said she was to have her hair trimmed by a real hairdresser, it was getting so thin and straggerly, it was not often brushed. It was the first time I had been without any grown-ups and I felt very important waiting on the platform for the little train that connected the town with about four villages, we always called the train Puffing Billy, it was so slow, a boy once fell out, he was not hurt at all, he just got up and ran after the train, he caught the drivers attention, and the train was stopped and the boy continued his journey, thats the kind of train it was;

We did our shopping and had tea at a teashop, that was another adventure, we had buttered toast and chocolate cake with cream, then it was time to go to the hairdresser, we had made an appointment when we first arrived, a beautiful girl with masses of red hair had written Kathleens name in a large book. When we got there, Kathleen was put in a chair rather like a dentists, dressed in an eligant blue smock and her hair was combed by a neat little man, after he had struggled with the tangles for a time, he gave it up and asked how we wanted her hair cut, so I said 'Oh, cut it long' Then I sat admiring all the beautiful bottles and things there were on shelves, we had never been to a hairdresser before. I glanced at Kathleen to see how she was getting on, to my horror I saw he had cut her hair almost to the bone, anyway it was above her ears, I begged him to stop at once, but he said he couldn't leave it half long and half short, in any case I had asked him to cut it long and that was what he had done, he pointed to the long chestnut curls lying on the floor, poor Kathleen saw them and grasped for the first time what had happened, she went quite green and fainted right away. When she came to she was frightfully sick, the disgusted man looked at it and said 'been eating chocolate I presume' It was all perfectly frightful, and even worse when we got home, Mammy was simply furious, and told Kathleen she looked like a little freak and her ears stuck out like the handles of a mug, that she was completely ruined and had better go to bed where no one could see such an eyesore. No one seemed to think her hair would ever grow again, poor Kay went to bed with her shorn hair in a paper bag, for many weeks she used to take her curls out and weep over them, unfortunaty her hair seemed to grow more glossy and a brighter colour after it had lived in a paper bag for a time, eventually Mary got so impatient with her she burnt it, but it was a long time before she got over the shock.

Funerals

We had some funerals in our family when people died, but it did not happen very often, we didn't go to the funerals or wear black, but some of our relations used to, they used to come back to our house and drink sherry and eat sponge fingers that were specially saved for funerals, I remember there was one old man called Uncle Roland, he has huge white maustaches, we only saw him when people died, he said he had not been to such a jolly funeral as Grannies for years. When it was time to go the relations used to take roots and cuttings from the garden, and it really was quite jolly because it was nice to know we hadn't any dead people in our house any more. Jimmy the dog eat the stuffed bird off Great Aunt Clara's hat, that caused a little unpleasantness, but after she had been presented with a few tree peony roots she forgave us.

Poor Granny, we couldn't help being rather relieved she was dead, she had been so bad tempered and difficult the last year or two, even more than usual, and the last three months we had to take it in turns to sit in her room, and what with the smell and her bitterness at being old and terror of being dead, it was awfully grim. She was allowed out of bed for a few hours each day, she used to sit by the fire with her nighty all up, and I was so frit of her legs which showed all shiney and swolden under her nightdress, I had to keep looking at mine to make sure they were not getting the same, they were rather fat. She had tiny feet and even when she was a fat old woman only took size three, but during the last year they had grown huge. She was very proud of her feet and we used always to know her footsteps, because they went such a sharp little trit trot, rather like the sound of pigs hoofs. Now they were so large with dropsy she had to wear Daddy's bedroom slippers all slit at the sides. Granny did not like us to leave her alone at all, she refused to have a nurse and when we left her to have our meals she used to tap the floor with a great stick, thump, THUMP, it would go on the diningroom ceiling, then if noone went up to her she would ring a huge school bell, the governesses used to have to tell us when it was lesson time, I can't think who gave her all those banging and clanking things. Often she would start bell ringing in the night, Daddy used to go and see how she was getting on now and again, but if she woke up and found no one there, clang, clang she would go until someone went to her, the first time it happened we thought it was a leper. When we got to her room she would make us rub her back for hours, my arm would ache so, sometimes I would go and wake Mammy and try and make her come and do a bit of rubbing, but she would pretend she was still asleep how ever hard I shook her, or if at last I did wake her by pinching, she would refuse to look at my hands, although a light was always burning in her room, she was frit of ghosts, trying to wake

Mammy was just as hard as rubbing Grannies back, anyway by that time she would have started her frightful bellringing again, there was only one thing that settled her, that was to go downstairs in the awful darkness over all those stone floors and fetch her a glass of neat whiskey, she was too weak to get downstairs herself. Now I am grown up myself I sometimes think all that bell business and back rubbing was a kind of blackmail, Daddy gave her a large bottle of whiskey each Saturday and it was usually Thursday and Friday nights she was ill.

The day she died, she got out of bed and sat by her fire as usual, but she kept shivvering all the time, she would keep asking for ginger pop too, I was sitting with her at the time, so sent one of the maids out for some, she drank two bottles straight off, the glass made a clinking noise against her teeth, she was shaking so, it was strange not asking for brandy or something warming, I'd never seen her drink pop before, she looked so wierd sitting with her legs all wide apart, a bottle in one hand and a glass in the other, shivering and shaking away, I felt afraid and asked them to send for the old Doctor, although it wasn't his usual day for a visit, When he came he packed her off to bed with several hot water bottles, but still she shivered and said she was cold, he said there was nothing we could do except make her comfortable, she was dieing. It was not my turn to sit with her again until late in the afternoon, I cast a frightened glance at the bed as I entered the room, there Granny lay, but they had done her hair in a little knob at the back, not all piled up on the cushions of old hair as she always wore it, even in bed, I hoped she couldn't see herself in the wardrobe mirror, her mouth was all smeared with dried cocoa, it looked awful, like dried blood on her white pinched face, her eyes were open, she could not see, she could talk though, she said her leg hurt, so I pulled the bedclothes down and saw she had burnt her leg on one of the hot water bottles, I put some vacellene on the burn, I didn't like doing it, but she said no more about her leg hurting so it must have been a good thing to do. There did not seem to be much else I could do to help so I sat by the fire and read *Tom Brown's Schooldays*, but found I was reading the same words over and over again, then she said she would like to feel velvet in her hands, she kept saying this so I gave her her old black velvet frock to feel and she seemed to like it. She asked me if I was reading, and said it was bad for my eyes to read in the dark, then she went on to say she thought one of the pleasantest things to do in the world was to sit in a swing, eating an apple, reading, when she was a girl her father wouldn't let them read novels, so she and Aunt Eva used to hide in their four poster with the curtains drawn and read *Wuthering Heights* and *Paul and Vigina* with a candle. That was the last reasonable thing she ever said to me and soon it was Beatrix's turn to sit with her and I excaped, all this put me off dieing.

In the night I awoke to hear the old Doctor and Daddy talking on the landing, I wondered sleepily what it was all about and got out of bed and looked out of the window, it was just beginning to get light, then I heard the Bacon Cock crow, Mrs Fenn is dead, Mrs Fenn is dead and she was.

The morning of the funeral the maids kept saying, You must go and say good bye to your Granny, it isn't right that you shouldnt and frightful bad luck will happen if you don't, even Mammy said we must. So although we were terrified, we did eventually, I quite expected to see a skeleton or a ghost in a shroud in a great black box, but what we did see was Granny looking quite twenty years younger, not in a coffin at all, but a thing shaped rather like a grandfathers clock, a shell they said it was called, she was all tucked in with fluffy cotton wool, sprinkled with daphne flowers and snowdrops, I was glad I had seen her like that.

Banishing smell and ghosts

When Granny was dead, Mammy said Beatrix and I could share her room, not share it with Granny of course, with each other, well I think I have said before what Granny's room was like, it simply smelt awful, worse than a thousands badgers, and was all stuck up with homemade lotions, the furniture was the worst kind of Edwardian monstrosity, made of yellowish veneered wood, humbugs, hair and fullers earth were stuck in all the corners of the drawers, the whole room seemed over-poweringly filled with Grannys' presence, and was most proberly stiff with ghosts. We explained all this to Mammy, and asked her to let us have new furniture and carpet and a little bed each, how could we sleep in the ghastly bed she had died in? we remembered the nights we had spent crouching in that bed rubbing her back while she rocked backward and for-ward groaning, and how she had lain dieing with cocoa stains round her lips. Mammy said it would be a very nice room when once it was springcleaned, and in any case, she couldn't offord new furniture, she just refused to discuss the matter any further.

We decided the best thing we could do would be to sell

every thing in the room without anyone knowing, I don't know how we thought we could smuggle enormouse wardrobes etc. down the stairs and out of the house, but we had very high hopes of doing so. After we had made this discision the next thing to do was to find someone who would buy this nightmarish junk, there was Lily the cook (the one who had illegitamate twins) sister, she often bought our old clothes and junk we found in the engine room, but she couldn't offord much, there was someone else we had business dealings with – Percy the fishman, he used to give us a shilling each for cucumbers we took from the greenhouse, we thought this a very fare price, so perhaps he would pay large sums for Edwardian bedroom suites, he was just about to marry so it seemed a good opportunity and it was. The next time he called at the house for orders, we enticed the bewildered man upstairs and bewitched him into saying he would be delighted to buy everything in the room if Daddy agreed, would £40 be a fair offer, we said it would and hurried him down to Daddy who was writing in the billard-room. We were a little alarmed about Daddys' reactions to our business deal, but he took it very well and soon Percy took the wretched stuff away. Mammy said we had been deceitful, all the same we were allowed to choose the new furnishings, so we had white furniture, white walls and a white carpet with a border of oak leaves, the ghosts and smell were banished for ever. Some time later we had to give the room up because Chloe needed it to have rhumatic fever in and I had to sleep in the passage room which was dark and damp.

Dampness and Illness

Our house was very damp and smelt of wallnuts and church, and floods were always coming, they covered most of the garden and we would walk in the water on our stilts. The cottage where the governess used to sleep used to be completely surounded by water during the Spring floods, Palmer used to have to rescue the poor old things in a boat, the cellers under the house used to fill with water and there were wells under all the kitchen floors, so one could always feel damp although there were huge fires, we didn't mind the damp but used to get rather a lot of colds and coughs, we liked having colds and staying in bed with a fire and lots of books, and no lessons to do. Kathleen had a beautiful croupy cough that was always coming, when I had a cough I used to pretend it was much worse than it was and strain myself to make an awful horse croak, but one of the maids called Florrie told me she used to work in an infermany, and an old man there kept coughing away, and up came his lung and she slipped on it in the dark, so I didn't try to cough any more after that.

When we had not got colds there were plenty of things like

measles and chickenpox to have, there always seemed to be someone in the family with measles, the Grownups didn't get ill very often, Daddy did once get a stroke and go stiff all down one side, but he came loose again quite soon, the parrot missed him so much while he was ill it died, and we had a funeral, the next parrot wasn't very nice, it smelt, Kathleen was supposed to clean it but she didn't.

About Trees

Most of the apple trees in the garden were Blenhems, there were a few Worcester Permains and cooking apples, but mostly Blenhems. One of the apple trees was called Smiling Mary, they were the first to appear, and we so welcomed them, and used to knock them down with a boat hook before they were ripe. There were several pear trees, one used to have a particularly plentiful crop of small sweet pears that were very bad keepers, so we let the village children have the windfalls, and the ones off the tree we picked and sold to Mrs Gould, we were allowed to keep the money ourselves. You had to go down steps to Mrs Goulds shop, she was very fat because it was too much bother to climb the steps to leave the shop, the local market gardeners sold her the produce they had left on their hands or rather carts after the market, her vegetables and fruit looked very limp.

Over the coach house there was a loft where the apples lived, they were very neatly packed on racks by Palmer and Daddy, Daddy enjoyed this Autumn job and was proud of the apple room when it was all finished, it was a beautiful sight, all those apples, and smelt heavenly. They lasted well into the spring, although we thought nothing of eating ten one after another, Chloe and I always eat the whole apple, core pips and every thing, I still do when I'm alone. I hate the kind of people who peel apples.

We had a medler tree too, the medlers were nice to eat, we liked the bitter taste, I used to make little bonfires with dry leaves and cook them in tins, the medler tree went the best colour of any in the autumn. I think we loved the wallnut tree best of all, we were all crazy about nuts, it was nice to get up early before anyone else, and look for wallnuts that had been blown down in the night, there were always plenty and our hands got all stained for weeks, at first they came down in their bright green jackets, and then in black or quite undressed, there is something so clean about a nut or conker that has just come out of its outer shell.

There were a lot of beech trees in the yard by the kitchen window, one looked like a woman and I thought she had been changed into a tree by a witch, I was always respectful to that tree, one had at sometime had a chain put around it, now the chain had cut right into the bark, all you could see was just the chain pattern, we would eat the beechnuts when there wasn't anything better to eat but they made our throats rather huskey.

The Field that was stiff with skeletons

Shortly before I left school some workmen were digging in a field near our house, they dug rather deep, up came some soil, stones then bones, then whole skeletons, 'There has been a murder here' they said, the policeman was called, he scratched his head and said 'It looks as if you are right' but they were wrong, when experts came they declared it was an Angelo Saxon burial ground, and they knew they were right because they went on digging and found the field was simply stiff with skeletons and they had nice little pots, beads and all sorts of things buried with them. People from all over the country came to look at our 'Skells' as we called them, they gave us a new interest in life, and for several summers the excavating went on, we became very friendly with the proffessors and we often brought them home for meals, Mammy was pleased about this as they wern't all old men, Daddy liked them too, but he was a bit worried about disturbing all those dead people, he very much dislike finding odd human bones about the house, they had a habbit of getting tucked down the sides of the morning-room chairs, they wern't white like ordinary bones, but rather brownish and soft, the dogs didn't like them awfully, which was a good thing because the proffessors would have been most annoyed if they had caught them devouring their precious relics.

One summer morning we were all at the 'skells' as usual, sitting with our legs hanging down the latest discovered grave, when a middle aged man accompanied by a boy of about fourteen crossed the field, they looked at the relics and spoke to one of the proffessors who was a friend of theirs, they were father and son, both were very dark and delicate looking, afterwards I heard they were dieing of consumption, I remembered the boy for a long time, he had such sad, shining brown eyes and a huskey voice, for some time I wondered if he was dead yet, but he wasn't, in fact he is still alive today, this I know because some years later I married him.

About the time they started unearthing all those skeletons Daddys' money affairs took a very downward trend, he thought perhaps it was due to them in some way, he forbade us to have any more human bones (except the ones that grew in us) in the house, but we still brought them home when we could steal them, only being more careful to keep them out of sight. One evening he was sitting smoking a peaceful pipe in the morning-room, he reached for a matchbox from the mantlepiece, but when he opened it, it wasn't matches at all, but toe bones, he was furious, and hurried down to the river and hurled them in.

Then an awful thing happened! During the night the river burst its banks up by the lock, when we awoke there was hardly any river left, just a muddy stream flowing down the middle.

Daddy was more frit of Angelo Saxon remains than ever, but we thought the river broken rather fun, for one thing no trippers came to the village any more, and there were village fetes, pony races, plays, jumble sales and dances held to try and raise enough money to mend the river banks again, when they did at last repair the damage, it broke down a few days later, as a result of using such cheap materials, so there had to be masses more jumble sales and dances, even Daddy who felt rather responsible gave a flower show in the garden. Everyone who was not too poor was expected to buy tickets for the dances, as the grown-ups hadn't been to a dance for about fifteen years, and Mary flatly refused to go, it fell to Beatrix and I to use the tickets, we were really much too young to go, but our parents never understood about things like that, we were only fifteen and sixteen, we were taken to the dances by another family, but when once we got there they didn't trouble much about us, and we had to stay right until the very last dance, because Wilkes used to bring us all back together.

At first we were so thrilled at the idea of going to dances so young, but soon we hated it, they used to have those awful programes with little pencils attached, how difficult they were to fill, nobody wanted to dance with us much, a few middle aged men took pity on us, and young shy boys who were too shy to ask real people, they danced with us sometimes, nearly always I had to spend the supper dance in the lav, besides the disgrace I felt dreadfully sad about missing the beautiful food. When anyone did talk or dance with me I used to be so grateful, sometimes tears would come into my eyes, other times I would chatter away so much they looked quite bewildered, and they would ask me if I would remind repeating all that again as they hadn't heard me quite distinctly.

We were both quite pretty, but our frocks were grim, they were made by the local dressmaker who lived in a tin hut in the middle of some allotments, all the dresses she made were kind of magya arrangements, very loose and hanging in lumpy folds, whatever pattern you took they were always the same, over these feeble looking frocks we wore evening cloaks of Mammys' made of flame velvet or brocade, they may have been alright on Mammy, but looked mad on us, our dance slippers were the kind children wear for dancing classes, with crossed elastic. I don't think it was only the fault of our clothes and youth we were partnerless, but local people were kind of frightened of us, they didn't mind coming to the house for parties and tennis and things like that, but the younger ones were frightfully rude and offhand and usually left with out saying thank you or even goodbye, the older people were more polite to us but rather dissaproving. Of course every one knew Daddy drank, but they thought we were all queer and there were many strange and untrue roumers floating around.

The morning after these beastly dances we had to show the grown-ups our programes and tell them what a wonderful time we had had and what a success we had been, it was an easy matter to fill our programes in and describe all the partners we had had, for some reason we dare not tell them what dismal failures we had been and how nearly everyone hated us, Mammy was always so impatient of anyone who wasnt a success, all the same she never did anything to help us to be one, she used to say if we didnt marry early she would be so ashamed of us, so we had that to worry about too.

After three summers they had dug up all the skeletons, at least all the ones they could find, anyway they were getting rather bored with ours, as another Angelo Saxon burial ground had turned up about ten miles away, I suppose if you come to think of it, England must be stiff with old disused burial grounds, only perhaps ours was in rather a good state of preservation, if ever I get a field of my own I'm going to dig very deep and see what I can find.

Before all the proffessors left they had an exhibition of some of the pottery, jewellery and just a few skulls, they had it at the Assembly rooms, lots of people came, including Marie Correli, Daddy found a funny piece of lace on the floor that looked just like her, so he mounted it on black velvet and placed her autograph which he tore off a letter, underneath, he always told people it was a piece of her knickers she had presented to him.

About Trees

There were three large lawns in the garden, the largest was used for tennis, croquet and occasionally bowles, the other had too many trees, mostly fruit, for there to be room to play games, but we liked apples and pears much better than boring ball games. One of the lawns was round and in the middle there was the enormous ash tree, where we did our lessons in summer and played, it was nice being in there, all greenish, like being under water. Once Beatrix and I thought it would be a good idea to keep tame frogs there, we put them in bird cages, it was not a success at all, they tried to get out, and got kind of squashed between the bars, and it was a horried sight, their eyes went all white, when we tried to help them they became even more squashed, it made an awful lump come in my throat, but the only thing we could do was to leave them like that, the next morning we went to the ash tree, expecting to see them dead, but they had all disapeared so maybe they recovered.

We loved all the trees in the garden, each one had a special charm, it was easy to climb, or an owl lived in it, some had branches particularly suitable for building houses in, small round things like pennies came off one, we used them for brewing dolls beer, there was one that had large red catkins that smelt of glue in the spring, I don't know what kind it was, but it used to russel like anything just before a thunder storm, for some reason only known to men, Daddy had most of it cut down, the next day Granny was looking out of her bedroom window, and there was the tree again, rather shadowy, but quite clear, when she told people they said it was the sun drawing the sap up from the trunk and it still went in its accustomed channels, so perhaps that is true and it wasn't a ghost after all.

The garden was particularly beautiful in the Spring, when all the bloosom was out, I seem to remember walking ankle deep in fallen bloosom, but thats exageration maybe, we used to make whistles with a piece of split bloosom, that the only way I can whistle still, I cant snap my fingers either.

During the summer we often did our lessons under the ash tree, it was a particularly fine one, its drooping branches touched the ground all round, except in one place where they were trained back to form a door, inside there was a gentle green twilight, the roof was made of beautiful twisting branches like snakes, we did our lessons at a long tressel table, they seemed quite plesant and not so worrying as usual. At times we had our tea here too, all the food looked faintly green.

Sometimes we would persuade Palmer to bring our dolls house down from the engin room and place it under the ash tree, it did not get damaged by the weather because it was so sheltered there, only the heavist rain penetrated through the leafy roof. Celeldines grew very thickly on the ground, we

163

would dig them up and use their roots for dolls potoas, boiling them over a night-light, they tasted rather bitter, we also fried cofee beans in candle fat, they were sausages, we used to fry dead minows too, they smelt just like real frying fish.

Spring Cleaning

Spring cleaning in our house used to last about six weeks, it usually started the week after Easter, Mammy dashed about in a large overall and cap, she gave everyone orders which she forgot in the middle of explaining what she required doing, and then told who ever was listening to do something quite different, she got frightfully worked up about it all and spoke in ghasps, we had to have what she called 'a fresco' meals in the conservotory or billard room, they were very elaborate and made an enormous amount of work, but the maids didn't grumble much, they rather liked Spring cleaning as their mothers were often roped in to help, they used to bring their youngest children hanging on their skirts, sometimes they turned out to be the maids' children, instead of their little brothers and sisters, the decorators also had their meals in the kitchen, so it was very gay in there.

Daddy throughly entered into Spring cleaning, and was as cracked about it as Mammy, only Granny hated it, she was terrified in case an invaison of paper hangers, mops and brooms arrived in her room, she spent most of the time guarding it, she didn't like the 'a fresco' meals much, sometimes she was expected to use cushions instead of chairs and on one occasion to eat salmon mainaise in the coach house.

The herald of Spring cleaning was coming down to breakfast one morning to discover the stair carpet had vanished, it stayed up for the duration, I don't know where it dissapeared to, then one by one the dining-room, drawing-room and morning-room and all the bedroom carpets were taken up and beaten, they were hung from two tall trees on a complicated kind of pully arrangement, and beaten by Daddy, Palmer and his son Jimmy, we stood as near as we could watching the piles of dirt that came out, I always get a kind of homesick feeling when I hear carpets being beaten, even now. The scarlet carpet from the morning-room was so worn out it was all white in places, once Daddy made Beatrix and I paint the worn places with red ink, one of Nellys' puppies drank the ink and was frightfuly sick, but it niether went pink or died.

The head decoratior was called Bacon, he had a beard and a hair lip, he also had an air of mystory, partly due to the fact that his wife was insane, she used to wander out side her house in 'The Blocks', she used to talk to us if we were passing, at first we were afraid, but she had such a sad, gentle voice we soon got used to her, she would weep and wring her hands, her gray hair straggled all around her, on the top was a hat with large black funeral plumes, her clothes were black too, trailing and old fashioned, but her face was quite handsome and except that her eyes were rather wild, it wasn't mad atall. It was something about a piano she was always trying to tell us, but she cried so much we could never make out what it was all about, either she had lost one, or had never had one but wanted to, she made us feel dreadfully sad, we hoped Bacon was kind to her.

Daddy used to clean the boot-room himself, and polish all his hundred boots and shoes to an even greater brilliance than usual, any shoes not quite up to standard were weeded out. He had a finger in every Spring cleaning pie, then he suddenly died, before the cleaning was half done, the next morning all the carpets were back in their usual places, and that was the last Spring clean we ever had.

'It'

One summer afternoon Mary was lying in the hammock, Beatrix had a grudge against her, so she quiertly unhooked it, down she went with an awful crack, she was simply furious, but Beatrix and I just laughed, it was so seldom we managed to score off Mary, when she got up we saw all blood on her frock, at the back, so we ran and hid till we were hungry. When we came out of hiding Mary said we had nearly killed her, and that she was very ill and we had got to treat her very well in future, then she said she had a great secret which she might tell Beatrix later on, it depended how she behaved, I was too young to be told.

Eventually all this passed out of my mind untill the same thing happened to Beatrix although she hadn't fallen out of any thing. She cried a lot, but all the same I could tell she was rather proud. After this once a month she would say in an awed voice 'I've got IT again' So we always called this strange happening 'It' Beatrix also started to develope a bust and hairs came on her body, none of these things happened to me, I was the same as I'd always been, I didn't want the hair but would have rather liked a bust. I told her I thought the hair frightful and no one would like or ever marry her if they knew she looked like that, so she grew very sad about it and one evening she hid in the spareroom cupboard and cut it all off with nail sissers, but it all grew back again.

When we were very young we used to think our brests were places that had come through Granny kissing us, we thought it was something to do with the sticking out moles she had on her face; We also believed we came out of eggs Mammy had hatched, there was an ostridge egg in a glass case in the drawingroom, we thought it was an addled baby that had never properly hatched, but might one day, we hoped it wouldn't

London visits and dieing babies

Every June there used to be a lot of quarreling between the grown-ups because Mammy wanted to go to London, Daddy had only been three times in his life and he hated it and couldn't bear any of his family to go near it, I think it must have been because no one knew him there which made him feel unimportant, but Mammy loved London so much. She always insisted on going during the season because she said it was empty at other times, I really think she thought all the business closed down and the shops only did a mail order trade as soon as the season ended. She liked to go to the more expensive Soho restaurants and took it for granted that all the other customers were fameous stage people or writers and artists. On Sunday morning she would wear an entirely new outfit and walk in Hyde Park, she said it was called Church Parade to do this, she could not understand why all society was not there, she expected to see the park stiff with men in top hats bowing to beautiful, eligant women. Sunday afternoon was devoted to the Zoo, a doctor friend gave us tickets, again she was disipointed, she hoped to see distinguished fellows of the Zoological Society strolling about with their families and a few other very grand people, but all we ever saw were rather a lot of servants enjoying their free afternoon and other very ordinary people. I think she must have got her ideas about London from reading rather poor novels when she was a young girl, but although she went there quite often she never changed them.

At one time she used to take Mary and Beatrix with her each year, Daddy would not let her go by herself, but Mary had the same opinion of London as Daddy, so when I was older I went in her place, but only twice, the first time when I was fifteen and again a year later. Before I went Mammy fed me with her views about London and I was expecting all the houses to be made of white marble and the streets to be as wide as the fierce part of the river by the weir. I was deeply shocked by the dirty slums backing on to the railway as we came by train to Paddington, but as soon as we left the station in a taxi (the first I had ever been in) I knew I would love London in spite of the dirt, I think the thing that impressed me most was the boys roller skating on the shiny tarred roads in the dusk.

Before one of these London visits Mammy used to write to the largest hotels for booklets and she would read and discuss these for days, but eventually she would stay with Maria Jones, an old friend of Grannies, but Maria was getting a bit dead by my time, so we went to a friend of hers who kept a refined boarding house in Bayswater, 1890 must have been our land-lady's heyday and she had never changed her style of dressing or general makeup since, next door there lived a mad man who used to walk round his little garden barking like a dog, but we did not see him often.

Although Mammy could not hear she used to take us to plays and musical comedies and she enjoyed films because they were not talking ones then. One evening Beatrix wanted to go to the Queens Hall and I thought it would be a good idea too, but Mammy drew the line at that and went to see some Black Magic almost next door. We had seats behind the orchestra and I hoped that people would think I was part of it, I held my hands down low so that they could not see I was not beating a drum or something useful. Although I was not musical like Beatrix, I enjoyed the concert very much it was the first real music I had heard. We were both feeling very happy when we came out into the main hall to meet Mammy as we had arranged, then we saw her talking to a very scared porter, and she was waving an umbrella and looking very fierce, it was a minute or two before we dared claim her, when we did she said she had been waiting for us for hours, and if Sir Henry Wood had gone on any longer she would have forced her way in and hit him with her umbrella, she had made several attempts to do this but the porter had stopped her. We managed to get her away and calm her a little, there were still plenty of buses to Bayswater, but every evening it was the same, she always left the theatres before the end because she was so frightened of missing the last bus, she had no idea how to get a taxi unless someone phoned for one, of course she couldn't whistle with her sticking out teeth but she could have waved her dreadful umbrella. One evening we did get her to go home by underground but she was too scared to get off the moving staircase and kept screaming and running up backwards, eventually a large workman came to her assistance and lifted her off. Beatrix and I were most ashamed, so many people had collected to watch, but Mammy rather liked the situation now she was safe, and kept explaining in a high pitched voice how she had never been on a moving staircase before, and when we asked her to come away on our hands the people said 'Look, poor thing, she has dumb daughters'

My second visit to London came to an ubrupt end, after we had been away a week, a letter came from home to say Chloe did not seem too well, Mammy said it was only a trick of Daddies to try and make her come home, but two days later a telegram came to say she was very ill with rhumatic fever, as soon as she had read it Mammy started to scream and cry, she said it was all Daddies fault because three of his brothers had died of it and it must be in his family. If Mammy had lived in the eighteenth century she would have swooned when things went wrong, it would have been so much better. As it was she ran down to the Edwardian Landlady and told her her youngest child was dieing and we must all go home at once, she left Beatrix and the landlady packing, while she dragged me with her to enquire about trains, we could have phoned but that wouldn't do atall, all the way in the bus Mammy kept saying 'My baby, my baby, my baby is dieing' and the other passangers were most sympathetic, the whole bus was almost crying, I kept trying to tell them we hadn't any dieing babies, just Chloe who was eleven and she wasn't dieing, only ill, but they hushed me up and said I was a heartless girl, strange women kept holding Mammy's hands and patting her. When we had made our enquiries at Paddington I managed to secure a taxi so the journey back was more peaceful, but we had dieing babies all the way back in the train.

When we eventually reached home we found Chloe really was very ill, she had been moved into the room I usually shared with Beatrix, because her own was very dark and damp, it was called the passage room because the maids used to carry jugs of hot water and things through it as a short cut, Beatrix and I had to sleep there now. The grown-ups said I had better go to Hillersdon for a few weeks while the house was in such an upheaval, there was a trained nurse and all kind of things going on. The nurse was most shocked about how matted Chloes long black hair was, but now it was all brushed and in two sleek plats, she had grown so clean and thin and remote she seemed like a stranger.

After a few days at home the Hillersdon people came and took me back with them in the car, the dressmaker who lived in the tin hut sourrounded by allotments had made me a frightful brown frock (Mary's choice) I had a large brown hat to go with it, I knew the frock was awful as soon as I wore it the first evening because Aunt Teana said how nice it was, the hat couldn't have been so bad because they took it away, they said it was too old for me, Aunt Eva produced an old trilby of Great Granddaddy's for me to wear, she usually kept it in the hall to scare burgulars, they were most angry with me when I refused to wear it, they kept trying to cram it on my head, the batty cousin kept hopping about with her camera trying to get a photograph of me in it, generally I was so frit at Hillersdon I did what I was told but I did stand out about Great Granddaddys' hat.

After a month of this kind of thing I came home, Chloes' rhumatic fever had gone, so had the nurse, but Chloe had got a weak heart now and it had a murmer in it, so she just lay in bed and looked very beautiful and ill. For a whole year she stayed like that, at first she was very fashionable with the grownups, but quite soon they got bored with her and she must have been very lonely although Kathleen sat with her quite often when she was not doing her lessons, that was one thing she was glad about, not having any lessons to do. When at last the doctor said it would be safe for her to get up a little we had two surprises, she had grown as tall as Mary while she had been in bed and of course none of her old clothes would fit also she was so weak she could not stand or walk at all, it was nearly another year before she could use her legs, for some reason Daddy was dreadfully shocked and angry about this and thought it was a disgrace. Poor Chloe she would sit for hours in an old fashioned bath chair that had belonged to Mrs Timpson before she died, she was put on the top path so that we could hear her if she wanted any thing, not Mrs Timpson – Chloe. There she would sit for hours, I would see her through the french windows of the morning-room as I sat by the fire reading or drawing, she sat all drooping and lifeless in her bath chair like a snowdrop.

Sisters by the Sea

Uncle Fred had a wife with funny feet, she kept them in black kid boots and walked with a stick, she said she got feet like that because a wicked man stepped on them but Mammy said it was heredity, anyway they got worse and worse as she got older and looked like seals flappers. She had lots of other illnesses the matter with her too, and her face was twisted with fretfulness, she whined and moaned at Fred all day, he looked like Daddy but was much smaller and tamer, they lived in Torquay because it was good for her health. Mary and I went to stay with them once, she had taken rather a fancy to Mary on her last visit to our house, I think she was shocked Mammy took so little interest in her, she made Mammy buy her some black lace frocks, she said she had married her daughters off in no time because they wore things like that. Mary had her own ideas about marrage, but she was glad to have some new clothes even if they were only made of lace.

We very seldom went to the sea, because there were so many of us and we lived so far away being right in the middle of England like that, we often longed to go, so were very glad to be going on a visit to the Freds although we didn't like them. Mary was twenty at the time, she had twisted her plats round her ears, but she had a lot of trouble with them, I was only sixteen and finding life very dull and difficult, no doubt I was dull and difficult myself, sixteen is a frightful age to be.

It was a very long journey to Torquay but when we did arrive we found Uncle Fred on the station, he put us in an open carriage with our luggage and we drove very slowly so that he could show us how grand Torquay was, he was a very boastful man. When we reached his home we found they were living in a furnished flat, it was the first time we had been in one, and it seemed very strange, for one thing the kitchen was in the middle of the flat and although it was made almost entirely of frosted glass, there was no window that opened, so there were rather a lot of cooking smells about, the food seemed queer too, we were not used to shop jam and marmalaid, and ready cooked foods, every thing tasted dry, and the things that were cooked at home had a very odd taste, we discovered why, Aunt Fred was very germ concious, she used to have the meat and fish washed in disinfectant before it was cooked, the milk always had to be boiled, even the flower vases had to have fresh water every day in case some germs hatched in them. She kept asking us questions about the housekeeping at home, then she would be shocked by how dirty we were and tell Uncle Fred, he got rather bored and said 'They are all Barbarians my dear, I shouldn't worry about it'

Aunt Fred didn't like Mary so much when she saw more of her, for one thing she could feel she was scornful of the shoddy way they lived, also Mary developed a large and painful blister

177

on her heel and insisted on wearing one bedroom slipper when she went out, she didn't like that at all, although it didn't look half as bad as the seals flappers.

Although he thought we were Barbarians Uncle Fred tried to be kind to us, he used to take us for sedate walks, to show us the beauties of Torquay, he was very proud of it and spoke about the town as if it was a foreign country, he wouldn't let us go on the beach and explore and look for shells and seaweed, and all the lovely things that grow by the sea, sometimes we had to sit and listen to the band, we hated it, but I couldn't bring myself to say so to him because it would make him so sad, there was something very pathetic about Uncle Fred.

The weather became very warm and sunny so we insisted on having a bathe, the Freds were very much against it but eventually gave in, Uncle Fred took us to a place called Paignton to have it, the beach was very crowded, we enjoyed our bathe, but we were only allowed a few minutes in case we caught 'our death' Unfortunatly the next morning Mary had a sore throat, she pretended to eat her breakfast and managed to slip out afterwards and get some throat pastels, her throat still hurt though. The next morning it was so bad she could not get up, I had to tell Aunt Fred who of course said that is what comes of bathing, she loved having doctors about the house so she sent for one in case it was something catching. Then the most frightful thing happened, the doctor said she had diptheria, Aunt Fred nearly went mad and her red hair came down (it wasn't real hair, only dyed) She pleaded with the doctor not to let anyone know such a disgrace had come upon her, Fred did his best to comfort her and I felt very shy and in the way as if it was my fault. Within an hour Mary was being put in an Ambulance, it was sad to see her being carried down the stairs, her face all gray. When she had gone the doctor gave me an injection in my arm, it made me feel rather giddy for a few moments, when I recovered I went to help Aunt Fred and discovered her in the bathroom, she was in her eliment battling with germs, all Mary's clothes, including her coat and black lace frocks were mixed up in the bath in a strong mixture of disinfectant, she did put the shoes in a separate bowl, I was glad Mary had gone before this deed was done, although I had been sleeping in the same room, my clothes excaped, but the room was all fumigated and sealed, as soon as it was unsealed I ran in and packed my clothes, I felt dreadfully homesick, they said I couldn't go home until they knew if I was going to have diptheria or not, but I refused to unpack my trunk, it gave me a feeling of freedom to know it was already to go home, Uncle Fred kept saying my clothes would turn to rope being left in a trunk like that, I would open it every now and then, half expecting to find there were only coils of rope inside.

I was allowed to go and see Mary in the nursing home where she had been taken, she was not very ill and fairly happy there, I didn't tell her what had happened to her clothes, it was very fortunate I didn't catch diptheria too because the nursing home was most expensive and there was a lot of trouble at home when the bill came. We didn't get invited to the Freds again.

Doom and Depression

An awful air of doom seemed to be hanging about, ever since I could remember there were wiffs of it every now and then, but as we grew older it grew with us until living in our house was like living in a fog, by the time Granny died when I was fourteen it was getting pretty strong and it increased more rapidly after that. Sometimes Daddy would shut himself up in the billard room and drink whiskey, quite often he would not come out again for two days, I suppose it was his excape, but instead of it making him happy he grew more and more depressed, it was always worse after the little auditor who smelt of pencils had been to stay. Mammy had her excape in her imaginary lovers, we children did not have much excape in the winter, but when the summer came there was the sun and river, some mornings I would get up at five and row up the river before anyone else had been on it, and the larks would be singing and the cows standing together in the little bays where the water was shallow, and everything would seem so good and clean, I felt I wanted to cry with so much hapiness, this feeling would sometimes stay with me all day.

Daddy was better in the summer too because he was so proud of the garden, when visitors came and he could show it off he was quite gay and Mammy too. There would be tea on the round lawn in front of the house, the tea would be laid on a tressel table with a huge white cloth on it, and there was homemade icecream and strawberries and lots of iced cakes with wasps flying around them. Mammy would be sitting at one end of the table and Daddy the other, and the visitors and us six children down the sides, and everyone would think what a happy lucky family and doom would seem miles away, but it never left us for long.

It was always with us much more during the winter, some evenings Daddy would sit by the morning-room fire biting his moustache in silent depression, Mammy opersite would be reading, the hand that was not holding the book would be held open towards the fierce fire, every few minutes she would close it as if to store the heat, when the monkey was alive it would sit between them doing the same. The air in the room would be thick and heavy, you could almost see dark cloudes hanging about, suddenly something would happen, Jimmy-the-dog would start franticly scratching his ear and yelping at the same time, (he had ear canker) Daddy would leap up swearing and kick poor Jimmy or throw him out of the French windows into the cold night, Mammy would start to scream and say he was ill treating her dog, but after a bit of quarreling they would sit down again and we would think it had blown over. Quite soon though Mammy would look over her book and say 'You Brute' and it would start all over again and last the rest of the evening. It wasn't always Jimmy-the-dog that started things, just anything when they were in that mood, other evenings Daddy would play billards with his friends and Mammy would sit by the fire wearing a tea gown trying to embroider something held over a small wooden hoop, it was always the same something.

Except at springcleaning times Mammy lost all interest in the house and the cupboards became full of dirt and rubbish and the larder sour milk and old joints with maggots in, ivy came over the windows and the house seemed to become more damp and there was a smell of mould and soot and mice about. No one mended Kathleen and Chloes' clothes, although I think it had always been like that, no one mending our clothes until we were old enough to do our own.

The maids got rather lazy too, they would sit over their meals for hours, sometimes they would all take the same evening off and just lay a cold supper before they went, we did not think of clearing away after we had finished, but just left all the dirty plates and half eaten food on the table for them to find in the morning, we never did a stroke of work. Mary sometimes sewed things with tiny stitches, but they were never quite finished, and Beatrix would play away at her violin if you could call that work, once a week a girl with a birthmark on her face would come and play the piano for her, and an old man with astma would play the cello, it sounded rather like a bumble bee the way he played, they used to do this in the drawingroom and while they were at it Mammy would put her head round the door and say 'Although we live in the country, we are cultured, not many girls have your opportunities' Mammy loved people coming to the house, but there were not many visitors now. There were a few young men who used to call and borrow our boats or tennis courts in the summer, she hoped they would fall in love with Mary but they wern't that kind of young man, in any case she was very haughty and scorned them.

As time went on Mammy lost heart more and more and her face began to have a blurred, dazed look, Daddy aged a lot too, although he was quite old it hadn't showed much before, I expect it was all the bills. He kept saying he was going to die, he said he looked forward to being dead and leaving all his depts behind.

Change

Right in the middle of Springcleaning Daddy died, it was sudden and awful. Beatrix and I were washing our hands in the bathroom, we were just going to Gorse Station to see if our new Guinea pigs had arrived, we thought it better to get them in the evening and have them well settled before Daddy discovered we had got them. Above the splashing of the taps there was a strange rushing sound, and there was Daddy running from his bed-room in his great white nightshirt and looking terrified, then he fell heavily down and made frightful snoring sounds, his face was all red and swolden, Beatrix screamed and Mary hearing her came and looked and looked, she kept whispering to herself, What is it, What is it. When we could move again Mary and Beatrix went to get help and I ran to fetch the Old Doctor who had helped hatch us all, now he was very old indeed – ninty seven I think. I ran so fast it only took ten minutes to reach his house, but when the maid opened the door to my frantic pealing of the bell, no words would come – just big ghasps, so she fetched the doctors' wife who at last gathered something of what I was trying to tell, she took me to the Old Doctor who was eating a late supper of spring onions and cheese, but he just wouldn't believe me when I told him Daddy was lieing on the landing outside his bedroom making those awful snoring sounds and nearly dead, he said 'Thats alright he will be quite well again in the morning, get Palmer to help him to bed.' Although I begged and begged him to come he would go on eating spring onions. Eventually to get rid of me he got his wife to phone his younger partner and he promised he would come at once, so I left the Old Doctors house for ever, and walked slowly home, dreading what might have happened in my absence. The house was very quiert, I found my sisters all sitting on the dining-room table in the deepest gloom, they told me Palmer and Jimmy had lifted Daddy back to bed and the doctor was with him now, then we realized no one had told Mammy what had happened, so I went in search of her, when I reached the main hall there she was coming out of the drawing-room with a letter in her hand, her mouth was all boxed up, then I remembered they had had one of their violent quarrels before dinner that evening, Mammy had had her meal later because she refused to sit at the same table with Daddy. She waved the letter at me hysterically, 'Here give this to that swine your father, this is to tell him I'm finished with him, yes finished, I'm going home, back to Hillersdon, No! I won't look at your hands, I hate you all, common little chits' I caught at her flapping hands and half dragged her up the stairs, then she seemed to understand something awful had happened and now begged me to tell her, her face was wet with tears of fright but I was too tierd to let her down gently she looked at my hands now, then screaming ran to the room she shared with Daddy, I don't know if she ever saw him alive because the doctor came to tell us he was dead a few moments later. It was as dark as a crows wing in the dining-room now, my sisters black henlike figures still perched on the table, I left them and walked down to the river, I sat on the swing, shocked and horrorfied as I was by Daddy's death, somehow I wasn't really sad, the last year had been a great strain, now everything would be different, it might be worse but it would be a change and surely more peaceful. I guessed tomorrow would be a frightful day, stiff with interferring relations, trying to plan our futures and talking about selling the house, throughly enjoying themselves at our expense.

In this surmise I was quite correct, relations came in swarms, all signs of Springcleaning vanished, when we came down in the morning all the carpets were back in their places as if by magic, although we had sent no teligrams all the relations came, again by magic, the Hillersdon people arrived first, the batty cousin had not forgotten her camera, then came Daddy's brother and his wife Auntie Fred, with her feet like a seals flappers, dyed red hair a harsh voice and the most fretful face I have ever seen, and the great Aunt whoes hat Jimmy-the-Dog had eaten when she came for Granny's funeral, this time she had a plainer hat with out birds, there were other shadowy people who didn't bring trunks, they wern't such a menace.

Awful conversations, if you could call them conversations went on like this – Well, Well, you girls, this will be the making of you, you will have to pull yourselves together and get jobs to keep your poor little mother, its pretty clear all your old father has left is depts, no money to train you I'm sure, you elder girls had better get posts as Mother's helps, Kathleen and Chloes' education will have to be continued at some village school, you will have to cut your coats accoording to your cloth, you know' Goodness it was frightful, they stopped all the newspapers and magazenes, sacked the maids, at least gave them a months notice, they didn't want the house to be servantless while they were still there, they poked their noses in the kitchen and gathered in to corners to say how extragavant we were, Aunt Clara pouring cream over her peaches, said she had discovered we had been having a pint a day, what shameful extragravance! Aunt Fred declared nothing had been washed at home for years, everything went to a hand laundry, hasterly she included all she could in the laundry basket, proberly telegraphed her daughters to send all their dirty clothes. Since Daddys' death Mammy had been in a kind of trance, we all felt rather limp too, the shock put all our periods out of gear, I didn't have mine for another six months, the maids said if that happens you would have a baby, it worried me a lot.

They were quite right about the money, the house would have to be sold to cover the Bank morgage, Daddys' lawyer came down and said we must put an advertisement in the newspapers asking people to send us their bills, it seemed rather an odd proceedure to us, but the creditors liked it and sent nearly £2,000 worth, the lawyer said when they were all paid there would be about £16 a month for Mammy and we must all get jobs, except Kathleen and Chloe, he suggested we were all trained to be shorthand typists, there might be enough money for that.

Poor Mammy, she just walked round and round the garden, they said she must wear black, so she wore a semi-evening frock it looked all wrong in the sunshine, we just went on wearing our usual summer homemade ginghams, I heard an old woman in the village say, 'Look at the husseys, not a shred of black between them' None of us went to the funeral.

When the guinea pigs arrived, we hadn't the heart to look at them, you cant take guinea pigs with you if you are a mothers help, these were beautiful ones with rosettes all over them, then there were all the dogs, who would look after them, my Firescreen Betty, what would happen to her?

When the relations thinned out, Aunt Eva was the last to leave, I think Mammy was a bit hurt no help was offered from that quarter, except the loan of Aunt Eva. When we were left alone, we all started doing things we didn't dare to do when Daddy was alive. Kathleen and Chloe just sacked the governess Miss Grove, and although they were only twelve and fourteen they never did any more lessons, Beatrix played the violin morning night and noon and quarreled with Mary all meal times, she did make arrangements to go to a Secretarial College in Birmingham, that was a senseable thing to do, I did my hair in a little bun, stole some of Mammy's face powder and let the dogs loose all over the garden to Palmer and Jimmy's fury, when Palmer swore at me I just swore back. But Mary was the boldist of all, for one thing she had her long black plates cut off, then she brought a black lurcher dog from some gypsies, who were camping in the Big Meadow, she called it

Zingaro, it was a perfectly dreadful dog, the short time she had it, it ripped the drawing-room curtains to shreds, killed most of the chickens and bit some of her Angora rabbits legs off. Then she took sixty pounds from her money in the bank and bought a cavervan with it, it was made of rather rotten wood, she said she would live in it till she either married or died, she still had £100 in the bank and said that would last her for years, but it didn't.

All the relations said we were to leave the house almost at once, even before it was sold, the lawyer agreed with this, and they rented a house for Mammy without even consulting her, she was in such a trance these days no one thought of asking her advice or treating her like a responsiable person. The house they took for her was a decaying farm house called 'The Gallow' about fifteen miles away, it had no sanitation, lighting or anything to reccomend it except that it was situated five miles away from any shops, which they hoped would keep Mammy from getting into fresh dept (this didn't work) The postman refused to deliver letters to such a god forsaken spot, when he reached the cart track that led to the house he blew a whistle and if you wanted your letters, you had to run down four muddy fields to receive them. Mammy had imagined she was going to a half timbered cottage with every convenience, the kind of place most of the widows in reduced circumstances she knew retired to, when the moving vans turned her loose with her furniture in her new home, she was so upset she really tore her hair like you read about in the bible or somewhere. Mary was already camping in the woods near, only Kathleen and Chloe lived in the house with her, they soon grew to like the life there and grew very fierce and wild, they carried huge sticks where ever they went and wore knives in their belts, Chloe quite recovered from being an invalid but Kathleen was still rather nervy.

Beatrix went to live with Great Aunt Clara on the outskirts of Birmingham, she went to a secretarial College every day, she quite liked learning shorthand and typing, also she was able to attend concerts, she had seldom been able to do this before, but living with Great Aunt Clara was grim and dreary, she sometimes went home to The Gallow for week-ends, but shouldn't think she enjoyed that much either.

I wished I could get a job of some sort and get away before the Sale, which would be a bit heart breaking, I felt already most of the furniture had Lot 1 etc. on it, also queer men with boiler hats had been to see us about probate or something, it meant we had to pay the goverment some money on the furniture although it had all been paid for many years ago, we said all the most valuable things belonged to Mammy so the goverment didn't make us pay for those because she wasn't dead.

It is difficult to get a job when you are only seventeen and have had no training of any sort, the things that interest me most, besides watching the strange things people did, were paintings, trying to paint, dogs, reading and lieing in a boat in the sun and fishing. I told Mrs Clare this and she said I wouldn't earn a living at any of these things except perhaps dogs, she advised me to try and get a job as kennel maid, so I put an advertisement in 'Our Dogs' all among Collie Chat, Sealyham sentiment, Bulldog Bites, 'Our Dogs' is a curious paper till you get used to it. I received a reply from a Miss Leary of Cornwall who had some dalmations that needed a kennel-maid, I answered her letter with great care and two days later a prepaid wire came, this is what it said:–

1. Are you a churchwoman
2. Are you a true dog lover
3. Are you a large eater
4. When can you come

To these questions I put the kind of answers she seemed to require and the job was mine, the eating question rather worried me at the time, but it was more of a worry when I really got to Cornwall, because the diet I was offered was mainly eggs, stinging nettles, blackberrys and thin porrage, the tea was dried and used time and time again, I used to eat the dogs biscuits without meat in when ever I could.

I sold most of my clothes to the maids and on the proceeds bought two white kennel coats and a ticket to Cornwall. No one with the exception of Mrs Clare took the least interest in my plans, Aunt Eva who had been telling us all we had got to earn our livings was furious when I told her I had actually got a post, she said I was the first rat to leave the sinking ship.

One awful morning I packed my few posessions, said good-bye to the house, garden, dogs and any of the family I could find and drove off with Mrs Clare in her new car which she now drove herself, to the station. I had the most beastly 'dancing class' feeling in my stomach and wished I was dead, but I didn't die, instead there I was crashing along in a smelly, cindery train, bound for 10/- a week, Miss Leary, Cornwall, dalmations and boiled stinging nettles, I was very much alone.

1st Dec 1941

Dear Barbara,

While I was staying with Connie I did take a day off and went to Shellford on my bicycle. It was awfully exciting, but sad too. Shellford is exactly the same as it used to be, and the only new houses are a few on the Gorse Road before you get to Gorse Court – only about fifteen altogether. But when I tried to find Shellford Court – honestly I couldn't at first. It has changed so much I thought it was another house. They have taken away the gates – all of them – and pulled down part of the wall and cut the ivy right away (it looks better without the ivy, or it would if the house was not such a wreck) you must never, never go and see it. Although some people are living there, the house is literally falling to pieces and it looks terrably slummy. Lots of the windows are broken and patched with bits of brown paper and even rags. The green houses are all broken and only skeletons of woodwork remain – the broken glass is left lying all over the place. When bits of the house fall down no one bothers to pick it up. It is a nightmare house. I climbed over the garden wall. The garden is just a field now and it is used as a chicken run. Nearly all the trees have been cut down or died and it is difficult to tell where anything was because there are no landmarks – just long, rough grass and mud. There is an evacuee mother and child living in the cottage the governesses used to sleep in, even this is all slummy now. I crept along the river path, most of this has fallen in the river – and I could see lights in the drawing-room and morning-room, and a very rough boy and girl came out of the french windows, they looked horrid and sulkey. The billard room is a school for evacuees, I think the house is a kind of boarding house.

The yard is a wreck with broken and ruined things lying all over the place – the potting shed is still standing but the greenhouse is in ruins and so is the stoke hole and other things. The stables are now Ladies and Gentlemens lavatories and the coach house is a shop and there is also a hairdressers in the apple room, the engin room is called Shellford court cafe. The kitchen has been rebuilt and is quite different.

The bridge is still beautiful and the river looks the same, but the pub, do you remember the white Lion? has been camouflagued and is all zig zaggy in a hideous brown and green.

The ash tree is still there but has had its branches cut much shorter, the little round tree the dogs were fed under has been taken right away.

I went to Gorse and Barton and Marlcliff and they are all exactly the same, also I went to Shellford Siding and the Road smelt of soot and cabbage just the same as it always did. I saw Palmer walking with two sticks looking very much as he always did too. I didn't like to talk to him because Mammy had a quarrel with him after we left the house, he was supposed to cartake but didn't or something like that. I also saw the old man with the red eyes who used to sweep the road, he used to look old when we were children, but he still looks the same, perhaps it is his beard. On the way to Barton there was ice on the roads and children were sliding on it like we used to, I saw a milk float with Wilkes written on it and an old man with a large nose driving it – so I suppose it was Wilkes. I did not see Botherem Dick or the Old Soldier, so they may be dead.

When I got back to Connies we looked through some acient documents about Warwickshire and found a deed of Shellford Court, the deed is dated fifteen hundred and something, so the house must be older than we thought, it is very sad to think how it is today.

I must finish this long letter now, my love to you and the children

Beatrix

THE VET'S DAUGHTER

Barbara Comyns

Introduced by Jane Gardam

'A wonderful and original novel' Alan Hollinghurst

Growing up in Edwardian south London, Alice Rowlands longs
for romance and excitement, for a release from a life that is dreary,
restrictive and lonely. Her father, a vet, is harsh and domineering;
his new girlfriend, brash and lascivious. Alice seeks refuge in
memories and fantasies, in her rapturous longing for Nicholas,
a handsome young sailor, and in the blossoming of what she
perceives as her occult powers. A series of strange events unfolds
that leads her, dressed in bridal white, to a scene of ecstatic
triumph and disaster among the crowds on Clapham Common.
The Vet's Daughter is a uniquely vivid, witty and
touching story of love and mystery.

'A small Gothic masterpiece . . . I have read it many times,
and with every re-read I marvel again at its many qualities –
its darkness, its strangeness, its humour, its sadness,
its startling images and twists of phrase'
Sarah Waters

OUR SPOONS CAME FROM WOOLWORTHS

Barbara Comyns

Introduced by Maggie O'Farrell

'I defy anyone to read the opening pages and not to be drawn in,
as I was … Quite simply, Comyns writes like no one else'
Maggie O'Farrell

Pretty, unworldly Sophia is twenty-one and hastily married to a
young painter called Charles. An artist's model with an eccentric
collection of pets, she is ill-equipped to cope with the bohemian
London of the 1930s, where poverty, babies (however much loved)
and husband conspire to torment her. Hoping to add some spice
to her life, Sophia takes up with Peregrine, a dismal, ageing
critic, but comes to regret her marriage and her affair alike.
However, virtue is more than its own reward, for repentance
brings an abrupt end to the cycle of unsold pictures,
unpaid bills and unwashed dishes. Barbara Comyns'
classic novel blends comedy and tragedy in
an unforgettable, bewitching tale.

virago

To buy any of our books and to find out more
about Virago Press and Virago Modern Classics,
our authors and titles, as well as events and
book club forum, visit our websites

www.virago.co.uk
www.littlebrown.co.uk

and follow us on Twitter

@ViragoBooks

To order any Virago titles p & p free in the UK,
please contact our mail order supplier on:

+ 44 (0)1832 737525

Customers not based in the UK should contact
the same number for appropriate postage
and packing costs.